MY JAPANESE WIFE

A Japanese Idyl

2nd Edition

Clive Holland

Originally Published in 1902

TABLE OF CONTENTS

Introduction

That the present edition of "My Japanese Wife" has been called for is a source of satisfaction to the writer. Of previous editions some 60,000 copies have been sold, and it is hoped the present version will prove none the less acceptable from the fact that the story has been revised and a considerable amount of new matter added to it.

The author has done this to enable the final form of the novel to be that in which it was originally written, but which for purposes of first publication in a particular series it was necessary to alter.

BOURNEMOUTH, ENGLAND. *April 2, 1902.*

Chapter I

Mousmé is leaning over me as I write. Mousmé, a butterfly from a far Eastern land, her dress of apricot silk, with a magenta satin obi (sash), a blot of bright colour in the dullness of my English study. My Mousmé! with Dresden-china tinted cheeks, and tiny ways; playing at life, as it always seems to me, with the dainty grace of Japan, that idealised doll's-house land. Mousmé, who goes with me everywhere, whose bizarre clothing attracts notice to her even when the delicately pretty face of a child-woman with innocent, soft eyes and finely arched brows is hidden behind the ever-present fan, which she draws from the ample folds of her obi.

My friends at Nagasaki told me that I was foolish to marry a mousmé, especially as I was to return to England so soon.

"Why not hire one for the remaining period of your stay?" suggested Kotmasu, who dined with me at my little toy-like villa so often that he began to offer advice as a matter of course. "Misawa would find you a mousmé," he continued, "whom you could put off as easily as an old glove. A real mousmé, not a geisha girl with a past, an ambiguous present, and a who-knows-what future."

Others of my friends laughed till they made the paper partitions of my house shiver like the strings and parchment of the samisen. "You will tire of her," said they.

Yet others with a knowing smile, "She will tire of you. They are all the same. Butterflies that change with the day. Moths which the night-air of reality blows to pieces."

But I would not be advised.

Advice is so cheap one seldom values it. Besides, had I not lived in Japan long enough to know what I was doing?

The only soul on earth who could have deterred me was Lou, that terrible sister who, before I had come out East, had formulated so many plans for my "settling down!" Who had selected—much as she would have a bonnet or a dress, and with almost as much care—several nice girls, any one of whom she had thought would make me a good wife. But Lou was thousands of miles away— how I revelled in that fact!—and would only be made wise after the event. Now as Mousmé is looking over me as I write—she knows as much English as I Japanese—I must set down how I met her.

It was one night at the Tea-house (chaya) of the Plum Grove. I had come up there with Kotmasu. The djins, bare-legged, panting runners, had rushed us along in the inevitable rikishas to this suburban resort up the hillside.

The town, illuminated with thousands of lanterns hung outside even the smallest of the houses, became, as we climbed upwards to our destination, a fairyland of colour and delight, as it always did at nightfall. In the silent waters of the harbour this gay scene was repeated by reflection in the glassy surface.

Upwards we went, Kotmasu and I; he calling to me every now and then, as his rikisha, spider-like phantom of a vehicle, was momentarily lost in the gloom to reappear just as suddenly in the patch of light thrown by some paper lantern swinging to mark the gateway of a villa retired from the road.

A Japanese night! Balmy, delicious; intoxicating with the odour of the flowers which came sweeping down on us in the breath of the mountain air, or creeping in varied scents over the hedges or toy-like fences of the gardens we passed; so soothing that Kotmasu, more used to the jolting of the rikisha than I, felt drowsy, and left off talking.

The sounds of the town, the music of guitars or samisens being played in the tea-houses or gaming-houses, had grown gradually indistinct and distant. Now scarcely any noise save the whirring chirp of the cicalas broke the still, sweet-scented air.

Soon we reached our goal, where I was fated to meet and be enslaved by the charms of Hyacinth—for so Mousmé was called. Above us, an inky mass against an indigo sky starred with points of light, rose the mountain, tree-clad, as I knew, on whose sides gleamed here and there the beams of light emanating from paper lanterns or paper-shuttered casements, marking the presence of houses or huts deep-set among the fantastic greenery of the woods.

"Will the sir get out?" exclaimed my djin respectfully, panting with the exertion of the ascent. I climbed down into the darkness, almost falling over Kotmasu, who had already alighted, laughing at our adventure.

Beside us, just where our rikishas had drawn up, was the ghostly gateway marking the entrance to the tea-garden, which lay at the top of a narrow path sloping upward; this wooden gateway painted Indian red and white, the white timbers showing like some spectral skeleton in the dusky gloom.

"Up there, sir," pointed my djin, who bowed low whilst acting as spokesman.

Telling them not to wait, because we should, as Kotmasu put it, "be many hours," we two entered the gateway, which marked the line of the palings of bamboo, and made our way up the narrow flower-bordered path to the chaya.

Through an avenue of sweet odours we walked, the mingled scent of tea-roses, gardenias and the soil making the atmosphere almost cloying with sweetness.

This wonderful garden of the tea-house, with its miniature ponds, bridges and grottoes, now all hidden in the darkness, was mysterious and even uncanny as all Eastern gardens are at dusk.

Set back a little from the path were serried ranks of sentinel-like sunflowers, of whose black, vacant faces, yellow-fringed, I felt conscious, staring at me out of the gloom.

A turn of the path and we were in a fairyland, whose existence none a hundred yards off would have suspected. Light for darkness; sounds in the place of silence.

We made our way beneath the paper lanterns of many hues, suspended in mid-air by slender, undistinguishable cords: dragons, green, yellow or red, as their bellying background of variegated paper demanded or the taste of the artist dictated, are there; and cats, monstrous and eccentric-limbed, such as provoke memories of such things drawn on slates in childhood's days.

There is a flood of yellow, orange, white and blue light on the paths and flower-beds stocked thick with asters, zinnias, strange fringed-edged ragged carnations and chrysanthemums, whilst bushes clipped and trained into fantastic shapes form climbing stations, so to speak, for huge and lesser convolvuli.

Through the paper shutters of the house itself stream more light and sounds of music played upon the samisen.

Kotmasu, a habitué, knocks upon the lacquer panel of the big door, which is speedily drawn back in its grooved-way. The wife of Takeakira the proprietor appears at the opening, a queer little old woman, silhouetted, with all the ugliness which so often comes with age, against a background of light; behind her a pretty attendant mousmé, just as if she was a figure taken from a vase. Both bow so low on recognising visitors that their faces touch the floor, and then they take off our shoes.

The mousmé conducts us upstairs, along a narrow passage, over the floor of which is stretched, stainless and wrinkleless, a matting of bamboo fibre, into a room which is bare and clean-looking almost to desperation and chilliness.

"Shibaraku," says the mousmé, addressing us both with a smile of welcome, as she leads the way, which speech Kotmasu tells me is meant for him, as well as the smile and show of white teeth between pretty red lips. Perhaps it is, "What a long time since you have been here!" being obviously inapplicable to me on a first visit.

The paper walls of the room—spotlessly clean—into which we are eventually ushered with a great amount of ceremonious bowing, are just like those in my own little doll's-house of a villa down in the outskirts of Nagasaki—mere sliding panels, each one in its own ingenious groove. And these by some wonderful process all fit into one another and mysteriously disappear. It is here we have to wait; in this bare room, with its long verandah running in front of it, from which "The Garden of a Thousand Lights," as its proprietor loved to call it, can be seen; and in the daytime the harbour, an irregular segment of the ocean beyond, calm, green, but animated by the presence of sampans—gondola-like, graceful, with indigo beaks and queer odd-shaped cabins—junks with sails of matting, traders of all nations, hulking colliers, and here and there a man-of-war belonging to a friendly or unfriendly Power.

We are given squares of matting on which to squat, in lieu of chairs, by the ever-smiling mousmé, who then stands mute, awaiting our orders.

"Are there no other guests?" asks Kotmasu, with a quick glance at the little standing figure.

"Yes, several," replies the mousmé, smiling. And, as though to verify her words, and dispel Kotmasu's enigmatic and somewhat incredulous smile, we hear unmistakable sounds of hilarity arising from the room beneath our feet, and from a distant chamber on our right.

"But," continued our mousmé, glancing curiously at me, and adjusting her obi of some flower-sprinkled material with minute care, "the English sirs mostly like to feast alone." Such was, at all events, Kotmasu's translation of the remark.

Kotmasu orders our repast; it is to be ultra-Japanese.

Sometimes at my own villa I regale him and seek to revive my own gastronomic memories with pseudo-European fare, which he pretends to like, but in reality loathes because of its immense portions—in the estimation of my Japanese chef; at these I always laugh because the meal seems so grotesquely disproportionate to one's needs—in Japan.

There is another reason than that so naïvely given—"the English sirs mostly care to feast alone"—by the almond-eyed mousmé; and Kotmasu explains it when the dainty little figure has disappeared through a sliding door to execute our orders. I must not set it down here. What is common and picturesque in Japan, is so unspeakable in English. Kotmasu sits silent, thinking of the meal to come, perhaps, in which "teal duck," raw spinach, raw shrimps, and even dog, were to find a place—all save the first, thank goodness, in minute proportions.

The sounds of revelry by night went on all the while that Kotmasu and I waited, coming to us softened and indistinct through chinks in the floor and through the paper panels forming the walls of the room—the voices of women and the accompanying music of the samisen, with its note of sadness. Then we heard the muffled sounds of the feet of geishas dancing, in their shoeless, gliding motions.

The strains of the monotonous music, punctuated with Japanese phrases, echoed in the bare passage outside.

Kotmasu got up and opened the door of grey paper leading on to the verandah, which had black and vermilion storks in flight across its two long panels.

We stepped out.

I for the first time; for Kotmasu I cannot answer. The sounds of the music became clearer, because the others had also slid back their paper doors, perhaps so that the sweet-scented air of the garden might enter, or a whiff of fresh night-wind from off the mountain come in to cool the breathless geishas.

The garden of a thousand lights, with its fountain of doll-like dimensions, in the lower and larger basin of which swim gold, silver and copper-hued fish, lies just beneath our verandah, and, after an artificial plateau, runs away down-hill into the darkness, following each side of the narrow, flower-edged path.

The paper lanterns with painted, bulging sides, some round, some like two mortar-boards of college days which had taken each other into partnership, some like elongated helmets of an Uhlan, and others like monstrous fishes, birds, or reptiles swimming and floating in ether, diffuse a soft, subdued light. A puff of air makes the whole lot swing to and fro so wildly, with a rustle of their paper emptiness, that Kotmasu and I are set wondering idly whether an immense lantern, meant to represent a gold-fish with vermilion fins and black vertebra, which is obviously troubled in its interior, will not flare up and hang, a blackened skeleton, amidst its gay companions.

A white cat flits ghost-like and silent-footed across the path and vanishes down it in answer to a dissonant call of its fellow, and in that moment the disaster happens. The gold-fish, which has regarded us with vacant vermilion-rimmed eyes, is instantly a mass of flame, and then, in another instant, a blackened travesty of a fish.

There are trees in the garden, also fantastic; green grotesques tended and trained with the minute care of a singular taste. There are little nooks, little rockeries in which strange toads and reptiles hide in the fresh moss and darkened crannies, coming out occasionally, sometimes to slip unawares or through ungainliness into miniature lakes—toy ponds—frightening the lazy gold-fish and making the water-lily buds and blossoms nod and curtsey in the ripples caused by their immersion.

The moon is rising, and the wall of blackness which begins where the lights of the garden end becomes gradually less inky, till at last, as the moon tops the mountain ridge, like some laborious and persistent climber, and floods the harbour with her pale, silver light, the vastness of the scene is disclosed.

Down below in the streets of the town the lights of art are paling in that of Nature's lantern. The harbour is a huge replica of the glass of frosted silver I bought last week in a curio-shop for twenty yen. The ships at anchor are mere spectres, narrow lines of ink, some of them with dots of light along their sides; the shadow of the hills, over which the moon peeps with cold, white face, just the breath on the glass as when a woman looks too closely into it.

The sounds of singing and dancing appear fewer now it is less sombre. Why does darkness exaggerate noise?

A steamer is going out; it is the mail, a thin thing like the match P. and O. boats I often swam in a bowl when a boy—the lights of her saloon mere glow-worms at this distance. But my companion must have seen all this many times before. Of course he has. And being more interested just now in "teal-duck" than the night side of Nature, he vanishes through the opened doorway, and I hear him drumming with his stockinged heel upon the floor to summon the mousmé.

"Ayakou!" sings out Kotmasu, who has sung "Hi! hi!" till there came an answering voice from below.

I leave my post on the verandah and enter the room, and along the passage at the back comes the sound of a mousmé pattering barefoot, her quick, short steps making a gentle thud, thud on the matting.

The panel door is thrust aside, and our attendant enters with a bow, and many ingenious excuses for the delay.

Chapter II

Kotmasu and I are seated; and on the floor before us our attendant mousmé places a wonderful bowl of seaweed soup—a dainty thing with sprays of chrysanthemums adorning its china-blue sides, the white-blue that you see in the eyes. To this soup I am used, and also to beans enshrined in sugar, and little fish equally astray from their proper element; but to the live fish, quivering its last quiver, perhaps, I cannot become accustomed, and even to watch Kotmasu—humane man in ordinary—placing the chop-stick impaled morsels in his mouth is almost too much for my still Western stomach. Of the "teal duck" and prawns I partake largely, making the mousmé laugh—so infectious are the emotions in this land of make-believe—by pretending to swallow the latter whole. I am not yet quite used to the chop-sticks, and occasionally fail ludicrously to spit my morsels, making both my companion and the mousmé roar, the latter clapping her pretty small hands with delight. But I am not annoyed; I have yet to see the foreigner who handles these strange implements better.

"It is not so easy as it looks," I say in excuse; and Kotmasu, with recollections of far worse performances than mine, agrees with me.

Our little dinner of toy-like viands, served by the soft-footed little mousmé, is gone through with fitting ceremoniousness, but at last it is finished, and Kotmasu is so pleased with the repast, that he is in no hurry for the long walk back to the town.

"There are generally pretty geishas here," he said to me, when we had lighted the ridiculous little pipes—mere tubes of silver, with a pigmy bowl at the end—which the mousmé had now brought us.

The jars placed before each of us, filled with sweet-scented tobacco of the colour of tow, and so "mild" that a baby might have inhaled its smoke; the spittoons and the porcelain stove containing the glowing embers at which we lit our pipes; always made me smile—they were so toy-like and minute—and long for my briar and honey-dew.

"Yes?" I replied interrogatively between the puffs. "Shall I tell Gazelle" (for such was the mousmé's poetic name) "to summon one?" he continued.

Why not? I had seen them many times before, it was true; but we were in no hurry, and they were always graceful, dainty, pretty and amusing—at least the best of them were, and no one troubled about those who were not.

"Is there dancing?" Kotmasu asked Gazelle, who had stood regarding us with a friendly look during our colloquy.

"Yes. Some of the best geishas from the town are here in the house. There is a party below, the most noble young Sen" (we had never heard of him, but no matter—it was but the mousmé's way of describing a good customer, who had probably kissed her pretty Dresden-china face and given her half a yen for the privilege) "is here with his most noble companions from the big ship. They have brought the geishas with them. They are dancing now. Listen! But doubtless I can get one to come for the pleasure of Mr. the English sir."

We nodded assent, and with a smile Gazelle vanished.

We heard the sound of the pad, pad of her footsteps retreating along the passage, then a sudden cessation of the noises in the room below, as we could imagine her opening the door. The zing, zing of the samisen suddenly ceased, and the girls' voices stopped their monotonous, chant-like song. Then came the sound of other voices seemingly in argument; then a recommencement of the previous noises as before our mousmé had interrupted the proceedings.

Then we hear Gazelle returning.

"Alone?" I suggest to my companion, who merely shakes his head and laughs, replying, "No. The geisha is light of foot—a butterfly, coming without sound, the heavy circling flutter of her fan like the beatings of the wings of the great grey moths outside there in the garden."

The footsteps of Gazelle came on, and then halted outside. There was no knocking at the door. How can one beat upon fragile paper panels with one's fist? And the usual little knocker of brass, a grotesque lizard, or miniature lion-head with bristling whiskers indicated and large white-balled eyes, was missing. The door-panel, with its flight of storks, and stiff but wonderfully realistic bed of rushes from which the storks had risen, was slid aside, and through the narrow opening the little dancing-girl fluttered softly in, like some gay-hued butterfly or large-winged night-moth.

"It is Snowflake!" exclaimed Kotmasu, and ere the dainty little figure bowed low before us, I caught a fleeting glance of recognition shot to him from beneath her drooped eyelids.

What a droll doll she is! Childish, with an assumption of innocence which is as charming as it must be unreal. An elegant, slender little figure, full of dainty grace. Her face painted—till it looked positively funny—its whiteness hiding the native transparency of her warm-hued skin, all damask rose and nut-brown tinted. And the two little dabs of rouge—oh! with what inartistic exactness they are placed, one on either cheek. The little rosebud of a mouth, with childishly pouting lips, is reddened brilliantly. And the delicate nostrils of her charming little nose—so piquant, so retroussé—are coloured just the same. Her jetty hair—somewhat coarse, I admit, but so glossy—is taken back from off her whitened brow, and lies in smooth, heavy coils on the shapely little head. A silver pin or two, and one of mother-of-pearl, with some charming baby-curls in rebellion on the nape of her slender neck, soften any severity.

And her dress. Plum-coloured brocade, with long pendent sleeves and a double tunic, the under one of a different stuff and very light, opening to disclose garments, such as her Western sisters are struggling for, of canary-coloured satin, vanishing into the curious tabi of white cotton, shoes and stockings all in one, with separated toes.

She was such a fairy-like little being, and her fan-play and posturing, which passes for dancing, so charming and graceful, that I could have watched her, as I have other geishas—soothed by the slumbrous pad, pad of her gliding steps upon the matting which covers the floor—almost all night. But at last she gracefully bowed, asked for her yen, and withdrew with the elegant fluttering motions of her class.

With the exit of Snowflake one became aware of the existence of time. Even Kotmasu was becoming drowsy. I could see through the open panels that the lanterns in the garden outside were going out one by one, beginning to give it a deserted look. The moon was on the wane, the white-faced moon in an indigo sky, and the walk home was a rather long one to which to look forward.

We rose, my companion very reluctant to go. The noise of the samisen still continued in the room beneath us, and the pad, pad of the dancers had begun again to the accompanying falsetto of the musicians' voices, in a strange monotonous chant.

We had paid the bill, mysterious items done in red ink upon a narrow strip of satin-like rice-paper; and so we went out by way of the verandah down the funny little steps which led from it to the garden path a dozen feet or less below.

We went down into the "garden of a thousand lights," and I idly counted those whose hearts were cold, whilst Kotmasu spoke to a friend.

"We are here!" said the friend, and in a little pagoda near a willow I caught a glimpse of others, a gay blot of colour in the half-shadow denoting the presence of ladies.

And thus was it that I found Mousmé and fell in love with her at first sight.

She, it appears, is the sister of Kotmasu's friend. In the subdued light of the little pagoda, where all the lanterns swinging to and fro in slight draught of air are yellow or red, I am introduced with marvellous ceremony to this radiant, childish being who is destined at once to captivate the heart and senses of the "English sir," as Kotmasu grandiloquently describes me.

She is clad in silks of extreme richness, and brocades which glitter with gold thread (for her family is a wealthy one), and her obi of turquoise-blue silk swathes her supple waist, and makes her look still more slender by reason of its exaggerated bow.

Her coiffure is pyramidical, the ebon-hued hair dressed à la butterfly. And the fantasy suits her; even the long, large-headed pins, which serve as mock antenna, seem appropriate to the queer grace of my mousmé. Her brilliant complexion is softened by the subdued light. Only her eyes sparkle innocently with interest.

Why had not Kotmasu presented me before? Was he about to relinquish his bachelor and somewhat erratic and amorous habits? The thought gave me quite a new sensation. Upon analysis I was forced to admit that it was jealousy. Miss Hyacinth (for that was Mousmé's name, I soon discovered), so fresh and delicate, a little figure off a tea-caddy, quaint and charming withal, had no doubt ensnared his vagrant affections, as she had my own admiration already.

Miss Hyacinth was addressing me in soft tones from behind her paper fan, which had pagodas, willows, and dainty little women like herself painted upon it.

Yes! I had been in Nagasaki a long time. I was English. No: England was not like Japan. Everything was larger, people ate more. There were no gardens like these, except sometimes when there was some grand feast taking place. This is but a tithe of the replies I made.

"Are the women pretty, and do they all wear rich clothing?" my mousmé inquired.

And I said "Some" in answer to the former, and earned a petulant moue. And "Not often" in reply to the latter, gaining thereby a smile of evident satisfaction as my reward; adding that "an ugly climate enforces ugly clothes." But I felt sorry almost on the instant, because she seemed not to understand.

"No paper lanterns at night! Is there then a moon?" with a look of wondering astonishment and apprehension.

"Yes!"

She seemed relieved.

"I have been to school," she explained, with a delicate assumption of dignity. "I have seen the map"—the Japanese maps are marvellous things, some of them—"I know where the mail-boats go. But there are so many countries in the way. How do they get there?"

All this in Japanese, of course, whilst Kotmasu talked to her brother in an undertone of the latest addition to the ranks of the Nagasaki geishas, a girl trained in Yeddo. And the other ladies sipped their tea and talked to the other men, who were nonentities to me.

Kotmasu had finished his jokes about the geishas, and became, perhaps, aware of my monopoly of Miss Hyacinth—whose name indicated a far less voyant flower than Western minds would associate with it—so he said, somewhat abruptly, "We must go."

For a moment Mousmé's small, shapely hand, with its cool, white fingers, rested in mine.

"I shake the hand English way," she explained, with a ripple of laughter. And then, with low bows to the other ladies, Kotmasu and I leave the merry party in the pagoda, and go away down the steep path bordered with the staring sunflowers.

I had read a few days before—and laughed at the idea—a line in a verse of a decadent poet that,

"Woman gone,

The darkness wraps us round in sable pall."

But now I did not laugh; I felt it, and understood.

I could have sworn that all the lanterns were extinguished, that the stars had gone down. And why? Because Kotmasu and I had turned our backs upon a pair of sparkling eyes, and I had put a hundred feet or so between me and Miss Hyacinth's beguiling, coquettish personality.

We don't talk much, and I switch absent-mindedly at the flowers with my toy cane of bamboo, as we pass along the narrow path towards the spectral gateway, now just visible at the bottom, a gaunt, white skeleton. Not till I send a big sunflower's head spinning off and up against my companion's legs, who starts as if something had bitten him, do I become aware that we have not spoken since we started down the hill.

Kotmasu pulls out his watch, a relic of his college days in England, and I waste a whole wax vesta—a luxury almost priceless in Japan, which I cling to—in enabling him to see the time.

Then we hurry out through the ghostly gateway on to the rough road, and thence onward down towards my house at as quick a rate as the obstruction of loose stones, sticks and ruts will let us.

Kotmasu shakes hands at my gateway. No, he wouldn't come in and have anything. Whisky saké would not tempt him, and "brantwein" was too much for his head, with still a good way down-hill yet to go.

My house had never seemed so lonely.

I fancied, strange though it may appear, that something—which after all had never existed—was missing. The tiny rooms seemed vast, the matting floor almost unfamiliar in its deadly silence.

The servants are at rest, of course. I think all I have to do is to push aside a panel and enter. There are no locks; and if there were, they would be but toy ones, ingenious, but useless all the same. I have a cash-box, a European one of tin, but I have given it a rice-paper jacket, because it looked so terribly substantial amid all my other frail belongings.

How lonely it is! Even Oka the cook's snoring down in the basement does not prove so companionable as usual.

As I cross the floor of my bedroom, and light the absurd little lamp near my apology for a couch, the dry boards of the thin flooring creak noisily and drearily beneath my tread. Some of the youthful fear of darkness is revived within me by the awful silence and the fitful flicker of my lamp. The little red-and-blue tortoises painted on the paper panels near the window seem to be coming to life and crawling about.

A glance out of the window as I throw off the last of my garments does not reassure me. Quite the reverse. It is so black outside. So I close the casement, and turn in sadly.

I lie thinking for some time in the dark, and almost insensibly my thoughts revert to our supper at the chaya of "A Thousand Lights" and to Kotmasu's friend.

A bright idea presents itself, solving my longing and loneliness.

It is Miss Hyacinth I want, and such a thing should not be impossible—in Japan.

Chapter III

Next morning when I look out of my window, whilst shaving in front of a "trade" glass I had obtained after some trouble for the express purpose, the view charms me with its vastness, just as the night before it had depressed me with its indefinable starlight gloom. "The view," I say to myself, "is the only big thing about Nagasaki."

Down below lay the harbour, bathed in Japanese sunlight, which—as even Japanese advertisements are beginning to put it—is like none other. On this particular morning it was filtering through a silver haze, and the water of the harbour looked like a solid block of chrysoprase with indigo shadows. In the distance one saw flaws in it where a sampan was, and white flecks where an incoming or outgoing foreign trader sailed.

What a network of narrow streets there was down below in the town proper! Narrow streets—most of which by now I knew—with slabs of stone laid in the middle of them, and in the older quarters, rickety houses nearly meeting overhead. It was down there that Kotmasu had his office, to which, however, owing to the industry and keenness of his merchant father before him, he was not very much tied. I had made up my mind to go and see him this morning, as he was usually to be found there in the forenoon.

It is pleasant to look upon the green hills, and even to watch the higher ones, bare and brown-topped, break through the fleecy mist hanging about their summits, as I have my breakfast on the verandah in the tiny cups and tinier plates and dishes in which my servants delight.

"Surely Mousmé—Miss Hyacinth" (I have got to call her this soon, in all conscience)—"will like my house," I speculate as I swallow beans in sugar, prunes in ditto, toy-sized cups of tea, and Huntly and Palmer's biscuits as my solid dish. She lives down there somewhere, nearer the town. I suddenly recollect Kotmasu once pointing out her brother Otiri to me, and telling me he lived somewhere over there. This must be better up here, and I remember quite gleefully that M'Kenzie, my chum, who died last New Year's Day, had found no difficulty in persuading a dainty little mousmé of equally good family to take him for better, for worse. I also recollect the circumstance of his having reddish hair, and an uncommon amount of freckles, even for a Scotsman, with amazing satisfaction. Because, although fair, I had neither of these things, and had even some pretensions to good looks.

I would go down and consult Kotmasu—that was the best thing to do.

I gulped down two or three tiny cups of tea, and hastily sought my hat.

Oka's wife was under the verandah, reeling silk off the cocoons on to strangely primitive wooden wheels, fixed between two upright pieces of wood stuck into a flat stone or cake of hardened, sun-baked clay for firmness. She rose, however, with a smile, and bowing, gave me one of my gayest paper umbrellas, "to match the morning." Strangely enough, the ground-work was of the colour of Mousmé's dress the night before. I used not to admire it greatly; now I wondered vaguely why.

I made my way down the hillside, striking the principal street or road after I left my own garden, in which camellias, gardenias, tea-roses and mimosa bloomed with such profusion, that the very air was scented and heavy with the mingled perfume.

It was a pretty garden—strange to European eyes, perhaps—with its make-believe fountains, toy bridges over equally miniature streams, and several tiny pagodas. It was pretty enough even for Miss Hyacinth, I thought, as I thrust open the quaint little rustic gate with my toe, and stepped out upon the road.

All the way down to Kotmasu's office I imagined, or tried to imagine, her flitting along the walks between the tea-roses and sunflowers. A dainty little figure in an elfin fairyland.

I had been down this way into the town scores of times before, of course, and the people knew me. The old man in the corner shop of the street, whose signboard was a queer mixture of Japanese and English of a sort, was painstakingly decorating the same large blue Nankin vase with sprays of chrysanthemums and the inevitable storks, as he was a week ago. But this morning I didn't stop, as I usually did, for a chat and to express my admiration for his painstaking art, which though almost totally lacking perspective, was yet quaint and pretty.

"No! I am in a hurry"—this to him.

"Is the sir going back to England?"

"No!" scarcely stopping.

"That is well! Good, good! The Nankin vases you, most illustrious sir, are so condescending as to admire are still unsold. Will you take them, honourable sir? They are——" All this I hear him say in his queer, cracked, high-pitched, monotonous voice ere I turn the corner.

"Yes, Mr. Kotmasu is in," replied San, my friend's clerk, and I could see him.

Kotmasu's office is a strange mixture of East and West. It is on the second floor of a warehouse, down on the Natoba near the water-side. He, with memories of English ways, has a writing-table made of mahogany, with camphor-wood and ebony inlaid work; but he still writes with a fine brush, either in Indian ink or vermilion, as the occasion requires, on dainty slips of flimsy and, to my Western mind, unbusiness-like rice paper.

How a London merchant would laugh at the idea of grinding up one's ink in a tiny saucer as one required it! And yet this is just what my good friend was doing when I entered—in a tiny jade saucer inlaid with threads of gold, with a minute bronze frog, just ready for a dive, upon the edge.

I sat down in a revolving chair, which had once graced the saloon of an English steamer lost along the coast, and opened fire upon Kotmasu concerning Miss Hyacinth.

I felt so miserably sure, with the pessimism of an ardent lover, that he must be in love with my darling. But it proved that he had no intentions. So much was evident to me after five minutes' talk in the cool room. He didn't want to chatter about her, but began instead to tell me untellable things about the new geisha. He didn't even seem to think Miss Hyacinth pretty. How strange, I thought! And then he went on again to sing the praises of the geisha, who was called Silver-Moon Face. His taste was evidently vitiated; he preferred art to nature, tricks to charms, a whitened face with two hectic spots of rouge, and the gold-lined lip, to the damask skin and smiles of my mousmé. But all this was very satisfactory to me, nevertheless.

I must have kept returning to the subject of Miss Hyacinth, for all at once he makes a discovery, and says without preamble, and as if certain in his own mind that he has "hit the right nail on the head"—

"Her people are rich, but still they might be induced to sell her."

"Man alive," I say, without remembering that Kotmasu's English does not extend to a knowledge of such a phrase, "what do you think I want?"

He is laconic, and smiles. "Hyacinth—the mousmé."

"Yes! but it is not for a temporary marriage"—I dress the phrase almost instinctively—"I want to marry her. Marry her as a wife, before the consul, or any one else, for that matter. Do you understand?"

Kotmasu's face is a study of simulated obtuseness.

At last, however, I make him understand, show him that I am in earnest.

Then he argues the matter in the politest Japanese, so as to magnify my "honourable position and name" as much as possible, and without detracting from that of Miss Hyacinth, show me my error.

But it is no use. I may be mad. We shall see, I tell him with an indwelling confidence; and he nods his head and remarks stolidly, "Yes, we shall see."

I should be angry with Kotmasu if I did not know that his opposition, like all the disagreeables of childhood, was intended "for my good."

In the end he promises to introduce me to my inamorata's family, and let circumstances rule the rest.

I go out into the sunlight, down the creaking outside stairs, quite light-hearted, and only haggle for ten minutes with Yen-kow the jeweller for a prospective engagement ring with a magnificent pink pearl.

I am sure as I leave the shop with the ring in my pocket that my weakness over the bargaining has lowered me fifty per cent. in the eyes of the stout little jeweller.

I go and buy some hyacinths, and then transact some of my business.

Kotmasu is coming to take me to see Mousmé at sundown.

I am at home again early in the afternoon, and, with a view to my proposed marriage, I begin to take stock of my surroundings.

I have lived long enough in Japan to see nothing exceptional in a marriage which will probably be concluded in a space of time that would be considered extremely short to a Western mind. The worst of it is, I am returning to England for good in less than nine months' time, and what will my people say to my choice?

I have neither mother nor father to reckon with. But I have a sister Lou, who, alas, is a dragon of propriety (and I am no St. George), who will, I fear, never realise that my wife is not an abstraction off a paper screen or a lacquer tray.

But then, after all, she will be my wife, and because she is pretty and "strange"—I fancy that's what Lou will call her—she may succeed in a society which, like the Athenians, is always running after some new thing. The latest "craze" is to my mind like a glass of sherbet. It creates the greatest amount of stir for the least space of time.

Not even thoughts of Lou, who is the pink of propriety—why isn't impropriety dubbed pink?—can terrify me from my purpose, because I am in love. I never felt so unafraid of Lou, her tongue and her smile, in all my life, even at the distance of many thousand miles, and I conclude therefrom that I must be terribly in earnest. As for the others, I don't care.

They have pleased themselves, have married as they wished, and surely may be reasonably expected to let me do the same, I argue.

My house, which seemed complete enough before, now appears only to require Miss Hyacinth's presence to make it all it should be.

I am very critical, but I can scarcely find anything to alter in my little home. My rooms at Cambridge, ere every one went in for Art—with a big A—talked Art, dreamed Art, abused Art, and outraged Art—were considered artistic, and my chambers in St. James' Street the same. It is in me, and has cropped out in many of the little details of my Japanese home. Clever and appreciative workmen and artificers have enabled me to see my desires carried into effect.

I play at having tea—imagining the while how the little white room, which is rather bare for European taste perhaps, but so clean, airy and spotless, will look with Mousmé in it; and then I go out on the verandah to wait till Kotmasu comes.

From my position I can overlook the road which runs away up alongside my boundary fence, higher and higher, till at last it vanishes amid the greenery and the tea-gardens. Down below, the older quarters of the town lie huddled together like a flock of sheep crushing each other in the endeavour to avoid some danger, swarming with people of the poorer class. It is not quite so fine an evening as last night was, and the hill-tops are hidden in the woolly masses of threatening clouds. The twilight is gloomy, and not orange-hued as before, and darkness comes more quickly upon its heels.

I light my treasured briar, and wait as patiently as may be for my friend.

When first I came here, how all my acquaintances used to laugh at the immense bowl of my pipe, which would, I should think, hold nearly ten times as much light-hued tobacco as theirs!

"Ah! Here he is at last!" I exclaim, discerning a dark mass approaching in the gloom, up the little narrow path.

"We will go at once?" I say questioningly.

"Yes," he replies. "They will be at home now."

We start off down the hillside, Kotmasu evidently from his remarks regarding the matter as a huge joke. If only he realized how sincere is my admiration for Miss Hyacinth. At last we reach our destination, and turn down a short road, which shuts the gaily-lit town still further below us from our view.

Miss Hyacinth is more charming than ever. Or is it the coming in from the gloom of the dark road, along which we have picked our way by the light of paper lanterns? She is quite delightful. She even knows a little English, which she learned at the school, so she tells me; and we talk together, I smiling inwardly at her funny phrasing.

"You speakee Japanese good," she says, with a glance from her sparkling eyes, and red lips wide open in her struggle with the last word.

I, of course, compliment her equally upon her English, which I assert is "wonderful," "charming."

This is all very interesting, and I more decidedly—most decidedly—wish to marry her.

I do not altogether like my mamma-in-law. But no doubt matters can be so arranged that my domestic peace will not be too frequently broken in upon, nor my artistic sense too often shocked by her puffy cheeks, inane smile and gimlet-hole eyes. To see her salute me—to witness the elevation of the immense bow of her dove-coloured silk obi as she bent to the floor—was too comical.

Mousmé gets nothing from her mother, I am glad to notice, except, perhaps, a certain almost indefinable womanliness, which all Japanese women seem to possess. It is almost as intangible as some of their perfumes.

I am offered tea in dainty doll's-house cups of blue egg-shell china, and smoke a ridiculous little pipe, because Miss Hyacinth prepared it for me, stuffing the tobacco into the tiny bowl with the tip of her small finger. She smoked, too, a little silver-mounted pipe, with a great deal of useless ornamentation on it; but refused my offer of a service like that rendered to me. She let me light it, however, with a bit of glowing charcoal, held in a pair of tongs which were formed by bronze lizards placed in the necessary acrobatic pose; and seemed pleased with the attention I paid her.

Mousmé, for so I begin to call her, has, it appears, several brothers and sisters; but I reflect placidly that if a man mustn't marry his grandmother, neither is he obliged, so to speak, to marry his wife's relations. Her little brother, Aki, a scrap of yellow humanity, with wonderful black eyes, and equally dark hair, is the only member of the family besides her mother present. And he—not yet at the enfant terrible stage of existence—regards me with curious but, I flatter myself, not unfriendly gaze, between bouts of playing with several minute bronze frogs and a box of dominoes.

Kotmasu keeps up an uninterrupted conversation in a rather grating undertone, whilst Miss Hyacinth and I chatter, and gradually get upon most friendly terms.

I am quite sure that she already thinks I wish to marry her. And possibly the only question now agitating her mind is, "For how long?"

Permanent marriages between Europeans and Japanese women are as infrequent as temporary ones are the reverse.

I am more than ever in love with Mousmé by the time of our departure, and am beginning to feel pained that I cannot relieve her mind as to my intentions being permanent. To do so will be quite possible without any breach of decorum in two or three days.

Kotmasu is full of the marriage, and as we walk homeward he tells me that Mousmé's mother will be delighted. He has at least commenced to arrange things, I think, with the celerity of a professed matrimonial broker.

"But," he said, "she is nevertheless surprised that you should not require Miss Hyacinth on trial."

"Did you say anything to her, then?" I ask in my surprise.

"It is all arranged, if you are willing," he answered, with some amount of pride at his successful diplomacy.

"But what about Miss Hyacinth herself?"

"She! Oh, she will be only too honoured to wed with the English sir."

How strange Mousmé's easy compliance with my wishes appears to me. But I accept Kotmasu's statement gratefully, for at least it relieves my anxiety.

I laugh quite light-heartedly; it is all so delightfully easy. And when I have had a smoke, after Kotmasu has drunk my health comically thrice over in whiskey saké and departed, I turn in and fall asleep, thinking that he is really a very good fellow.

Chapter IV

All has gone well, and I am to be married to-morrow. Kotmasu is to be best man, and for this purpose he has hunted out from the depths of his disused steamer-trunk an antiquated suit of Bond Street "morning attire," a relic of his stay in London; which, if less modern, is more correct than the creations of Kinew, the Anglo-Japanese tailor near the quay, who has a tendency, so I am told, to make his coats short in the waist.

Mousmé's mother is delighted—a state of mind perhaps not altogether unconnected with various handsome presents which faithful Kotmasu, who should be a member of the corps diplomatique, naïvely suggested my making her.

The marriage can be very easily contracted; and Kotmasu, who still seems to have little or no faith in my constancy, has assured me, over and over again, that if, after all, I should change my mind about taking Mousmé with me back to England, a few more handsome presents to Mousmé's mother, and the gift of a couple of hundred yen, with a handsome dress or two, to Mousmé herself, will simplify matters.

But I am vain enough to think that this is not so; and that the gleams of Western ideas which I have detected in Mousmé's conversations, picked up doubtless at the school, may cause liking to ripen into a lasting affection on her side, and be the forerunners of greater breadth of mind. There is a great deal of complexity about relationship in Japan, and I had long ago ceased to be surprised at anything in this way; but I received a mild shock on my wedding day when I discovered to what innumerable families—to say nothing of individuals—I had allied myself. In fact, I somewhat ruefully thought that I must be brother-in-law, son-in-law or grandson-in-law to half the Japanese population of Nagasaki.

The marriage company was a study—if I had been in the humour to make one—of all sorts and conditions of men, women, children and babies, all gathered together to do honour to the marriage of their kinswoman, Miss Hyacinth, with "the most honourable English sir."

Mousmé's mother was resplendent in one of my "handsome presents," and her compliments were interminable. She advanced smilingly to meet me, and remained in the same condition throughout the whole proceedings. I felt almost as nervous as I should have been expected to be had I contracted an aristocratic alliance in England, culminating in a smart wedding. I have very little recollection of the details of a day, or rather part of a day, which seemed to resolve itself into a series of oft-repeated salutations and endless congratulations, refreshments, smoke and discreetly repressed excitement.

At length it was over.

I had plucked my Hyacinth, and was free to lead her away to my home.

Mousmé in all her bridal finery of flowered satin gown, and obi of plum-coloured silk; Mousmé with the shy face, and pretty ways which might or might not be artificial.

I was to discover all this, perhaps, and many other things.

The legal formalities had been all previously arranged with the assistance of my excellent Kotmasu, who is a person of some importance, and of weight with the officials who attend to such matters.

There is really such a very little to do; so few things for Mousmé to transport to her new home; nearly all could be easily packed in a large Gladstone if she possessed such a thing. As it is, her belongings are brought up the hill to my house in an elaborately decorated lacquer box, by a big little brother with a bullet-head, nice eyes, and a great liking for teriyaki (plums in sugar coats). This box is a fit ornament for the boudoir of a princess, I think, as the youngster puts it down in a corner with a sigh, produced by aching arms.

I smile and fancy how Lou would laugh at a trousseau contained in a lacquer box measuring about 20 inches by 12 inches by 10 inches!—remembering that hers, which was described at portentous length and with unblushing detail in the columns of the Queen and Lady's Pictorial, must have occupied little short of six large Saratoga trunks. But what matter? This style of thing is a mere flaunting of wealth by Dives before the aching eyes of Lazarus. Even the wealthiest can only wear one dress at a time, and Mousmé can do this, and with far more grace than some of the salt of society.

As for Mousmé, she seems quite at home. She soon unpacks her tiny box; and, noticing that things connected with my toilet, such as my razors, hair-brushes, comb, and tin of shaving soap, are arranged near the window on an improvised dressing-table which was (when I first took the house) in reality an idol stand, she arranges hers there too. How queer they look, to be sure!

Alongside my shaving soap now stands a tiny lacquer pot with a jade lid, on which is carved a wonderfully pretty group of storks, containing the rouge which gives a delicate sunset flush to her cheeks. She puts a little on at once, right in front of me, as naturally as another woman might wash her hands, probably because she feels she must do something before a glass which is, as she puts it, "so big and great and bright," compared to those to which she has been accustomed. Then there is a little pot—also with a jade lid—containing a white face preparation, the use of which I shall at once inhibit; this she puts close beside the other by the force of association of ideas. The tiny brushes, with backs of tortoise-shell, the combs of the same, the hairpins with big eccentric knobs, are all placed near my gigantic brushes.

Then her few garments are taken from the box and hung—also like mine—on pegs which I have had put up on the wall near my mattress-like bed.

Mousmé is satisfied with her work, exclaiming, "Velly good ting that!" in the monotonous voice of a person speaking an unaccustomed tongue, and we are ready for our first meal.

She is pleased with herself, with me, with her new home, with everything. And after our dinner, during which she has chattered in most diverting English, learned at school from an "English teacher," anxious to please me, whom she still, I fear, looks upon as her owner, she proposes to sing.

What queer English it was!—often almost unrecognizable from mispronunciation. She still calls me "Mister," and almost makes me choke with smothered laughter each time.

Fully twenty minutes are occupied in attempts to master the appalling intricacies of "Cyril"—my name. The nearest approach as yet is "Cy-reel," which must do for the present, with lapses into "Mister" when she forgets.

Whilst I smoke, Mousmé sings songs in a soft little tone, to the accompaniment of her long-necked samisen.

She has a rather pretty voice, and more idea of expression than any other Japanese singer I have heard.

Night comes at last, and after a long look down from the verandah at the hundreds of lights gleaming far below, we go to rest upon the mattresses which Oka's wife has unrolled ready for us upon the floor; Mousmé with her head fixed into the groove of a block of mahogany, which serves her as a pillow, and preserves her wonderful erection of hair intact.

We are under a huge mosquito-net, of course—one of steel-blue gauze. When I first came I used to detest the confinement, and tried to do without it. But mosquitos are invincible, humanity frail, and the epidermis easily punctured. I returned to the protection of what I laughingly got to call "my meat-safe," after the second night.

Outside our tent-like mosquito-curtain we hear the angry buzzing of the foe; whilst big, heavy-winged moths every now and again come with a tiny thud against the enshrouding gauze, to dart away again towards the small, glowworm-like flame of the pendent lamp, which for no particular reason I always keep alight throughout the night.

When I awake next morning with the sunlight streaming in through one of the shutters, which the warmth of the previous night induced me to leave open, Mousmé is sleeping still, sleeping as peacefully as a child, her face wreathed in the smile of a happy dream, and her head still resting upon her little wooden pillow.

I creep out from beneath the environing curtain without disturbing her, after carefully reconnoitring lest one of the enemy should gain entrance.

I blow out the tiny flame of the lamp, which looks so horribly yellow and sickly in the daylight, put on my flannels, and go out into the garden.

I am going to get some flowers for Mousmé when she awakes. I cross one of the tiny bridges—spanning an equally tiny streamlet—which seem made only in children's size, and which creak complainingly beneath my tread, and make my way to the thicket of roses in which my soul delights. A big frog contemplates me with an offensively open stare for an instant, from the edge of the basin of the plashing fountain, before diving with outstretched hind-legs beneath the shining surface. The red-gold noses of the fish, which are poked just above the water as they nibble at the edges of the lily leaves, disappear instantly the surface is ruffled.

I gather a huge bunch of damask-petalled tea-roses, heavy with perfume, and smelling as attar never smells. As I go along the walk with the mossy edge, in which lizards and strangely beautiful beetles play hide-and-seek in the sun, in search of some gardenias, the stanzas of a native poet stray through my mind, commencing:

"The dew shines on the lily; and the rose opens her crimson heart to greet the rising sun."

I soon have my sprigs of gardenias mingled with the roses, and I return to the house, hoping to lay my offering by Mousmé's side ere she awakes.

I enter the strangely bare bedroom, with its gray panels and vermilion storks, from the verandah. A queer old idol, belonging to the former owner of the house, grins—there is no other word for an accurate description—benign approval from its pedestal in the corner. I had retained it because it filled a niche; because I have rather a penchant for curios; and lastly, because, as an irrepressible midshipman nephew once put it, "It's the jolliest-looking old idol I've ever seen—a combination of J. L. Toole and Madame Blavatsky."

Mousmé is still asleep when I enter, but the creaky floor awakes her ere I have half crossed it. She rubs her eyes in a somewhat bewildered fashion, and then with a smile promptly buries her little retroussé nose in the posy I have brought.

Then she rises from the mattress-like bed, a blue linen gowned little figure with tiny bare feet, and nails on them like rose leaves, and trots across the matting floor to a position in front of our improvised dressing-table.

She peers into the glass anxiously to see whether her slumbers have disturbed her hair, touches the thick, neatly-arranged plaits with deft fingers on either side of her smiling face, and then laughs at my amusement.

Mousmé's toilet is a very simple matter. She has few garments to put on, no hair to do, or rather no hair which wants doing, her elaborate coiffure being a permanent erection for some considerable time. She tells me that it took "nearly a large day to do it," and I quite believe her; it is such a wonderful erection.

All is so delightfully simple. She puts on her little patches of rouge—with a less reckless hand, in deference to my opinions on the subject—in a trice, puffs some white powder upon her cheeks and charmingly impudent nose, reddens her lips with the certitude of a practised hand, slips into her gown of flowered silk, and with a pretty little pleading moue entreats me to tie the enormous bow of her brilliantly coloured obi; and hey, presto! as the conjurer says, almost in less time than it takes a Western woman to put on her bonnet, Mousmé's toilet is complete, and she is ready for our make-believe playing at breakfast.

She eats her sugared plums with dainty grace, and drinks an astonishing number of cups of pale amber-coloured tea; but then the cups are so small that her doing so provokes little wonder in my mind. She has, perhaps, a misgiving that she has eaten more than I can afford, although I overheard my mother-in-law telling her that I was a very rich man; for she says, interrogatively, "I eat too great velly much? Not eat so again?"

I smilingly assure her that she is to eat as much as she can, and she laughs and gets up to attend to the flowers on the verandah, and place fresh blossoms in the blue china bowls which stand on eccentric perches on the walls, in the corners of the room, on a bamboo and lacquer cabinet, and on my English-pattern knee-hole writing-table in the window.

Mousmé has deft fingers and good taste, and the flowers seem to arrange themselves in negligently artistic masses beneath her touch.

She makes an exquisite picture as she flutters about in the bright sunshine of this white, airy room, in her dress of rich, gay colours.

I sit still, and desist from my mail letter to watch her. And as I do so, I become aware that a journalist who "did" Japan may be forgiven much for one true, picturesque phrase, "Japanese women are butterflies—with hearts."

The cicalas chirp unceasingly, making a natural orchestral accompaniment to her movements—the chirping cicalas, which seem to rest neither day nor night.

The only bowl still unfilled with flowers is that on the table at which I am sitting. Perhaps she is still too shy of me to touch it. A thought has evidently flitted through her pretty head, for she goes out on to the balcony, and a minute later I see her slender, quaint little figure going down one of the sunlit garden-walks, evidently in search of something. A lizard scuttles away across the path at her approach, to cower amongst the moss and tea-roses; and as she turns the corner towards the gold-fish pond, I catch a last glimpse of the huge, brilliant bow of her obi which I laboriously tied an hour or so before.

It is very pleasant to have my pretty little mousmé flitting about my home and garden. I wonder somewhat vaguely why her absence has never struck me before. Love apparently is one of those flavours of life which one misses least when one has not enjoyed its piquancy.

I take up the thread of my letter to Lou again. It is a thousand pities, I think as I do so, that I cannot present Mousmé to her some such bright morning as this, and in Japan. The rarest gem is best seen in its proper setting. How surprised Lou will be! She is large and fresh-coloured. There is sure to be an explosion. How well I know the sort of thing which is certain to occur! Her handsome face will redden, and the letter will be tossed across to Bob with a sharp, "How ridiculous of him! He really should think of us a little. I only hope he won't bring the woman here. Fancy a Japanese sister-in-law! Why, Bob, you're laughing! It's no laughing matter, I can assure you. A yellow-faced, painted scrap of a woman. There——" I can hear her in imagination saying all this, and in my mind's eye see her expression. Ah! Lou, I also remember that all your roses are not of Dame Nature's giving, and that others—malicious, no doubt—have remarked upon the fact.

I hear the patter of feet coming up the verandah steps. It is Mousmé returning. Ah! Mousmé, you and I will conquer London together! You with your dainty grace and piquant face, I with my wealth, as you esteem it, and family name.

Her hands are so full of flowers that she has to push aside the panel with one knee ere she can enter.

She comes across to my table and places the blossoms in the empty bowl of bronze.

By a stroke of genius in coquetry the flowers are hyacinths!

When she has finished their arrangement, she says smilingly, her lips parted, and twin rows of white pearls showing between them:

"They are me. You never forget me when you see them!"

"No! Mousmé, I never shall."

Chapter V

I have only seen Kotmasu once since our marriage, now five days ago; and then it was quite by accident, down near the quay, where I had gone to discover whether my quarterly parcel of magazines and books had arrived, which Lou with commendable regularity despatches "to that brother of mine who is out in Japan, living at one of those towns with a heathenish and unpronounceable name."

Kotmasu seemed somewhat surprised to see me.

"Where is Madame?" he asks with a smile, as though—as no doubt he did—he half suspected she had returned to her mother already.

I must have shown that I read the undercurrent of suggestion somewhat plainly. "At home," I answered. "You wouldn't surely expect me to bring her out at this part of the day, in all this heat, and down here, too!"

"No! no! Of course not," he hastened to reply.

I was somewhat mollified by his evident anxiety to put matters straight again between us. He can scarcely, I thought, be expected to have the same faith in my experiment as I have. To him my marriage, until it has existed for some time, can, I realize, only appear in the light of a temporary arrangement.

"Why do you not come up as you used?" I inquire in a friendly tone.

"It is your—what you call it?—something to do with the bees and the moon. I did not care to intrude," he replies deprecatingly.

"How ridiculous! We shall be always glad to see you, my good fellow," I reply, laughing as naturally as I can.

Kotmasu is so terribly English.

Even his attire this morning is that odd mixture of Anglo-Japanese garments he so much affects, consisting of a straw hat and tennis flannels, worn in conjunction with the flowered dressing-gown-like garment of a well-to-do merchant.

He looks a strange figure as he stands talking to me, in the sun, at the corner of the little narrow alley leading from the water-side into one of the newer streets, the incongruities of his garments thrown up into strong relief by a background formed by the sail of a large trading-junk alongside the quay, which a swarm of Japanese coolies, all dressed alike in tight hose and dark butcher's-blue cotton tunics, with some bizarre device in a different colour on the back, were unloading with extraordinary rapidity.

"I must go back to the warehouse," he says, after considering my remark. "I will come to see you to-night."

He shakes hands; and a coolie who has been staring at my "strange white face," as I overheard him call it, for at least five minutes, to the neglect of his work, appears much mystified by the supposed rite.

I am glad Kotmasu is coming, as I wish him to believe in my experiment as thoroughly as I do myself.

The books have come, and I return to the warehouse of my parcels-agent to see if they are unpacked.

Mr. Karu's office is always a source of wonder to me.

The amount of business transacted there, in a building of toy-like dimensions and fragile structure, was little less than marvellous.

Whenever a parcel heavier than usual was dropped on the floor by a careless coolie, I expected that the room, with its ink-stained, paper-panelled walls, on which were pasted or fixed with quaint-headed pins the steamship bills and those of several of the theatre tea-houses, would collapse forthwith with no more warning than the crack of its slight, dry timbers.

The parcel was ready.

Mr. Karu was all smiles. He was a little, short man with extremely beady eyes, quick movements, and a yellow skin deeply pitted by small-pox.

"It is very big to-day!" he exclaimed in Japanese, referring to the package. "Very much larger; half a yen more, please, most honourable gentleman," as I put down the usual amount.

The smiles were explained; and there was no doubt some truth, I thought, in what the little chief-clerk at the bank, who is so anxiously cultivating a beard, said, namely, "That most excellent friend, Karu, is in great much hurry to get much rich man."

I pay what I know to be in great part an imposition, with an indulgent grin—I am in a hurry to get back to Mousmé, or might have argued the matter even in this heat—accept the offer of a coolie to carry my parcel for the equivalent of three-halfpence, and start to climb up the shady side of the rough-paved street to my home.

Mousmé was waiting for me at the little gate in the toy fence of bamboo—a fence the like of which in no country save Japan would have been deemed sufficient for the purpose intended.

She came forward to be kissed (I had had to give her a few lessons in this custom) with her chin—which in the sunlight was as if carved out of ivory, so fine is the texture of her skin—tilted up, and the red rosebud mouth wreathed in a smile. Mousmé is learning European ways rapidly. My experiment seems very promising; and she is evidently growing very fond of me. She is learning English, and even the English alphabet, so books are becoming of interest to her, especially those with pictures in them.

"What is there?" she inquires eagerly in Japanese, pointing to the parcel which the coolie carries on ahead of us up the garden-walk.

"Books."

"Books? More books!"

My slender library, contained on shelves about five feet high and three feet six broad, appears illimitable to her.

"Yes," I replied, smiling.

"Are there pictures in them?"

"I expect so."

"Hi!" to the coolie staggering under the weight of the parcel. "Hayaku! Walk faster! Run!"

And then, almost before I know she has left my side, she is gone, hurrying with short steps up the moss-bordered walk after the coolie, who has quickened his pace into a shambling run.

By the time I reach the house at my slower rate, and enter my room by way of the balcony, she has already got the parcel in front of her on a square of white matting in a patch of brilliant sunshine.

The only fault I am able to find with Mousmé's face is that it is somewhat apathetic at times, a trifle expressionless. It is animated enough now, however. A look of eager curiosity suffuses it. She is like some gay-coloured humming-bird in her brilliant-hued dress, squatting there in the patch of sunlight, already at work with nimble, painstaking fingers upon the knots of the string around the parcel, coaxing loose the more stubborn ones with the point of one of her immense jade-topped hairpins.

Lou has sent some magazines this quarter which delight Mousmé immensely—The Strand, English Illustrated, and a copy of the Universal Review. This last is a veritable El Dorado of pictures, and provokes exclamations of delight when Mousmé turns the pages over. Only there is so much she cannot understand.

One particular picture in a number of the English Illustrated, a group of ladies at an evening party, mystifies her immensely.

"Why are all these women cut out in the middle?" she asks with a puzzled expression. "Are they all born like that?"

"No," I reply.

"Then do they make themselves like that?" glancing at her own slender though by no means exaggerated figure.

"Yes; they make themselves so, I suppose. It is a custom of our nation, and other European nations," I explain as best I can.

"Oh!" with another look at the ultra-fashionably slender figure of the woman in the foreground of the picture. "How very uncomfortable!"

We both laugh; I because Mousmé makes this last remark in such a finite voice, and without any real idea of its naïve truthfulness, and she because to her loose-robed little body such a fashion appears highly ridiculous.

There is evidently something mysterious about this funny custom, which, as Mousmé says, "makes women look as if a dog had bitten a great piece out of them, both sides;" for she says, ere turning over the page:

"Shall I do that when I go with you to England?"

"No, certainly not."

"Why?"

"Because you're much prettier as you are."

Mousmé smiles contentedly, and pats my big hand, which looks so very large beside hers, and rambles off to tell me of a lizard she found in our bed just before I came back from the town; whilst I, glancing over the pages of one of the magazines, divide my attention between her story and a critique of Robert Elsmere.

The time passes very quickly with Mousmé; she is soon tired of looking at books and papers which, at present, she only half understands; and lest she should interrupt me, she gets up, and goes with a hushed pad, pad of her shoeless feet into our bedroom, to fetch a strange little lacquer box which contains her writing materials. A flat shell, with lovely mother-of-pearl tints on its nacre hollow, in which she grinds her Indian ink; the fine paintbrush, which plays the part of pen; the flimsy rice-paper, in long, thin strips, and envelopes to match, are among her belongings, and are decorated with tiny pictures of trees and strangely grotesque animals, birds and fishes. She is going to write to her mother, to ask her to send up a sash of turquoise-blue silk which was left behind when she was married, and which she has found out I admired.

I watch her as she writes, her head bent over her paper, and the lower half of her face in shadow—such a scrap of daintily dressed femininity.

I wonder what else she is saying—women's inter-confidences are always so distressing and perplexing to a man—for she has already covered one long strip with delicately minute writing, which at a little distance looks like the ground-plan of an intricate maze; and surely even a turquoise silk obi cannot call for such a lengthy description, except, perhaps, in a Parisian fashion-journal.

She has finished by the time I have cut the pages of one of the novels Lou has included in the parcel; and, with a solemnity worthy of the best traditions of the Japanese official, she seals it up securely in an envelope of whitey-blue rice-paper—so small, that it necessitates the folding of the letter half a dozen times.

One of the ever-amiable Oka's almost innumerable children, a quaint toddler of five, with a queer, shaven head, with its little ebon queue, and small, bright, black beads of eyes, is easily persuaded to take it down to Mousmé's mother for a couple of sen. Then we have tea.

Really it is a sort of dinner, a nondescript meal best conveyed to the mind by that equally nondescript English phrase, "high tea"—a strange meal indulged in by people who are too hungry to have tea, and too modest to have a second dinner.

How Mousmé can tackle plums still green, though coated in sugar, without paying the penalty for her seeming indiscretion, is a mystery. But she does; and I sit and watch her in genuine though unexpressed admiration. The shrimps, really large prawns, with their intricately stuffed interiors, I can venture upon; and seaweed, with sweet sauce, I take with resignation. She does not care for the latter to-night, and so she goes to a panel cupboard, where we keep our priceless English biscuits cunningly hidden from the possible depredations of Oka's somewhat inquisitive children, and eats some of these instead, nibbling off first the pink-and-white sugar decorations, which are such a source of delight.

We have scarcely finished our meal, and Mousmé is still nibbling a biscuit, when we hear the sound of Kotmasu's expected footsteps coming up the garden-path.

Chapter VI

It is clear to me from Kotmasu's talk, glances, and conduct in general, that he has not yet got to consider Mousmé in the light of the mistress of the house. I am also sure that he even yet cannot understand that my marriage with her is anything more serious than a passing freak, a fancy of the hour.

He is very familiar with her, and she with him—they have known each other so long—chatting together quite freely. I am not jealous, surely; but I suddenly discover that it is time to go out. Kotmasu at once agrees that it is, and Mousmé seems delighted.

Where shall we go?

That is the all-important question, which is not easily settled.

Mousmé inclines to paying her mother a visit; Kotmasu to visiting a little play-house down below in Nagasaki, where some new geishas from Yeddo are to make their début.

I am not so fond of my mother-in-law as I should be, nor of my perplexingly numerous sisters and brothers-in-law, both small and great. The former I suspect of rapacity, an insatiable appetite for "handsome presents," which, if not always very costly in European eyes, are certainly numerous, and range from rouge fin (imported from Paris) and blanc perle to gay-hued obis and handsome hairpins of tortoise-shell, or of bronze with carved jade heads.

Fancy supplying one's mother-in-law with rouge! But it was Kotmasu's doing. He was evidently in her confidence; for he said one day, just as my marriage arrangements were nearing completion:

"You give Madame Choto some rouge. The woman very fond of it. You make her like you."

This being what I wished her to do, I did as friend Kotmasu desired, expending three yen (12s.) upon a box at Yan's, the best druggist in Nagasaki, and paying at least four times its original price. The only satisfaction I have is the knowledge that my mother-in-law's complexion is of the best!

Mousmé clearly is to-night all for going down to Madame Choto's, but I have one trump card to play against that. I am destined to find it in the future—as in the past—of great service. I have merely to say, "Let us go and look at the shops."

"Yes, yes," answers Mousmé with alacrity, clapping her small hands.

And so it is settled.

The recollection of Madame Choto and the little brothers and sisters she was half a minute ago so bent on visiting, speedily fades from her mind.

Kotmasu agrees readily enough, no doubt thinking that there is still a chance of our dropping in, later on, at the Willow Tree Theatre, to see the famous geishas from Yeddo.

To get down into the town at night is a matter of some difficulty, the path being so rough and unlighted. Of course, we carry lanterns—nearly every one does at night—and one constantly meets processions of families or friends, out either for a walk or on their way to some place of amusement, all carrying paper lanterns of various colours, and giving a pretty, fantastic effect to the dark roads and narrow streets of the town.

It is far more interesting to go down into the older quarter of the town, the true Japanese, if so I may call it—the native quarter unalloyed by European customs and commerce.

Mousmé leaves us for an instant to look out three paper lanterns with their slender, quivering carrying-sticks of bamboo. She at any rate is all eagerness to be off, visions of possible purchases for her personal adornment doubtless flitting through her mind.

It is nicer out under the verandah; the dry wood roof, in which the cicalas live a chirping existence, seems to be giving out the heat with which a thorough sun-baking has stored it during the day.

Kotmasu and I step out on to the balcony to await Mousmé's coming with the lanterns.

There is no moon to-night, and the clouds hang low, making the evening dull and close. Everything is so still, with a deep silence that is at once oppressive and slightly terrifying, until one is accustomed to it. Down below lies the town, like some vast black monster with many twinkling eyes. There is no wind; indeed, there is scarcely enough air to disperse the smoke of our cigars, the ends of which glow like the red eyes of some wild animal. I can just see Kotmasu's face when his glows brighter as he inhales.

"And you are not getting bored?" he asks, puffing a cloud of smoke amongst the foliage of a creeper trailing at his elbow.

I know what he means, although he mentions no name, because we are talking in Japanese, and Mousmé may even now be creeping silently, as is her wont, across the room behind us.

"No; I am charmed. She is even more charming than I thought. I shall certainly go home to England as soon as I can."

"And take her?"

"Certainly; why not?"

Kotmasu can on occasion be fairly concise, if not epigrammatic.

"Mousmé in Bond Street!" he ejaculated; and if he had been English, I knew instinctively that he would have whistled.

"Why Bond Street?" I asked somewhat feebly, with just a shade of chilliness at my heart from the incongruity conjured up by his words.

"Because," he replied slowly, "that would be a good test."

I might have attempted a reply, but there is a sudden glow of light on the verandah, a yellow-red, diffused light, which fails to pierce the gloom at the far end, and Mousmé and Oka appear with the lanterns.

Mousmé gives me a kiss, to the peril of her lantern with its monster of a crayfish painted in vermilion on its yellow side; at which Kotmasu smiles indulgently; then we start off.

We go away down our garden—which has such narrow paths, some of them scarcely less pigmy than those associated in my memory with the garden of childhood's days—now so dark and full of mysterious shadows, heavy with the strong scent of flowers, alive with the incessant noise of the cicalas, and movements of huge, soft-winged night-moths, which circle round the light of our lanterns, beating their wings with a soft, quick rattle against their distended sides, and every now and again flying into our faces and making Mousmé give a little scream of simulated terror, at which Kotmasu and I laugh.

I shut the gate after us, and then taking Mousmé's arm, we make our way down the rapidly sloping road. There is another party ahead of us, also with lanterns; and so steep is the path, that in the black darkness we almost seem as though we should step off into the abyss, right down on to the swaying lights below us.

Such strange shadows are set dancing on the road by the swaying lanterns we carry, that Mousmé, who must, after all, have seen such things dozens of times before, clings closer to me for protection, and in a low, frightened undertone she says:

"Cy-reel! Cy-reel! I am frightened! I shall shut my eyes and take hold of you!"

But when I look down at her a few paces further on, I see that it is but her delightful coquetry; for her dark-brown eyes, which in the lantern light have shadows like a lake, are open, and are watching Kotmasu, who is a little in advance of us two.

She catches sight of me, and bursts out laughing. She is never a bit ashamed of being caught like this.

When once we reach the bottom of the road, which runs past older houses even than mine, villas mostly inhabited by the better-class merchants and the few foreigners who may have protracted business in Nagasaki, we are plunged almost without transition or warning into the heart and life of the town.

We go along the street, brightly illuminated by hundreds of lanterns, pendent and ambulatory, at some small risk of being run over by rikishas taken at a rapid, nay, almost reckless pace by their active drawers.

Mousmé walks along quite gaily, her wooden clogs making a great clatter on the stones which crop up in the street, in concert with those of scores of other women who are out with husbands, brothers or escorts for an evening's amusement or stroll. She is so naïvely proud of her "English sir," who is a real husband after all.

We go through the streets, which at night seem all the same, all gaily lit with flaring oil-lamps, and illuminated with countless numbers of paper lanterns, which throw a mellow-coloured radiance on the faces of the passers-by; looking in this shop and that as we walk slowly along.

The sense of possession is very strong in Mousmé. Every now and again she clutches my hand or arm—though, strictly speaking, to do so is not Japanese etiquette—and fires off little nods to acquaintances. Every clutch at the sleeve of my coat means that she has caught sight of some one to whom she wishes to exhibit me as her real husband. When Kotmasu, who is a wonderful recounter of tales relating to those we meet and nod to, laughingly reproaches her with indecorousness, she says:

"What you say well enough; but I Engleesh now, you know," with a moue and a little quick turn of her dainty head, which makes both of us laugh, and the passers-by stare in astonishment at our sudden merriment.

Yes, Mousmé is so English—in everything except what really constitutes Englishness. What a revelation England will be to her, and she to my respected relatives!

These streets we walk through are wonderful. They are all alike; the houses, of frailest woodwork and paper panelling, are scarcely varied in any particular, save that of ornamentation, from one end of the long row to the other. There are no shop fronts, no glass windows; so that intending purchasers, or even those who have no intentions other than curiosity, can take up the various articles so openly displayed, and examine them at their leisure.

This is what Mousmé delights in doing. She likes best the shops in which rich dress fabrics and women's ornaments play an important part.

A tiny parcel, done up neatly in rice-paper, betrays the fact that she has already coaxed me into purchasing "a little present." The shopkeepers, who squat in the midst of their wares, offer no objection to Mousmé's inspection; and as it amuses her, why should I mind?

As we go along towards the lower and harbour end of the town, the crowd of people gets denser and denser. If the terrors of horses—Nagasaki is as guiltless of horses as Venice itself—driven or ridden, were added to the djin-harnessed rikishas, one would walk along at momentary risk of annihilation.

But the djins are wonderfully active and intelligent, and avoid obstacles with marvellous ability. There are few corns in Japan, and the wheel of a rikisha over one's feet, therefore, is of somewhat less moment.

Mousmé flutters along at my side, chattering in Japanese, and English of a sort, gay and contented, her sense of the ludicrous being aroused every now and then by the sight of one or other of her countrymen in the garb of civilization—Western civilization, that is. A Japanese in European attire in Europe may be an artistic mistake; in Japan an inartistic atrocity. There are several of these about, in out-of-date pot-hats, and tail-coats of the year before last's cut. Even Kotmasu, who himself is attached to pseudo-European attire, laughs at them. How queer they look!—the pot-hat cum a fringe of black, shining hair beneath its brim, and other really picturesque garments.

We are getting tired, and Mousmé's natural lust of buying useless things is increasing.

Unfortunately, she has been told I am "one very much rich man." Kotmasu—who is beginning to pine for the geishas—and I have our arms uncomfortably full of purchases——little lacquer boxes, fantastic hair-combs and pins, silk sashes, a tiny silver tobacco-pipe with tortoises, frogs and tiny lizards scarcely bigger than a pin's head crawling up the chased stem, boxes of plums preserved in sugar, and French bonbons purchased at a ruinous price. All this is very strange, and even Mousmé's recklessness is charming, captivating.

There is no time for the theatre now, so Mousmé and I make our way to a tea-house, and Kotmasu, who has been such a long-suffering companion of our peregrinations, goes off to see the geishas, and, I fear, a somewhat improper variety entertainment.

The chaya is full of its patrons. Such a crowd of mousmés and their escorts; and very few of the crimson-and-gold covered futons (cushions), which are negligently arranged for the use of the guests under the verandah overlooking the garden, are vacant. So we step out into the garden, and enter a quaintly constructed summer-house built to accommodate two.

We have scarcely seated ourselves, after my having drawn aside the paper shutters on the garden side, ere a charming little scrap of an attendant mousmé, with a dress of yellow silk and scarlet satin obi, presents herself to take our orders.

She stands in the lantern-light just outside the doorway, caressing her knees with her tiny hands, and smiling and showing her pretty teeth in anticipation of receiving a "good order."

After a hurried consultation with Mousmé, who says, "Sugar plums! Oranges! Tea!" the little gay-hued waitress flits away in search of what we have ordered.

The garden, of which the owner is so proud that he calls it that of "The Hundred Beautiful Lights," is a quaintly pretty one. Just behind our little summer-house, with its octagon roof of thin split laths of mahogany and paper shoji, with French-grey backgrounds adorned with country views by a local artist who has shamefully overlooked all the canons of perspective, are lotus-ponds—tiny, toy-like expanses of water in which doubtless the inevitable goldfish swim and mouth for air bubbles; miniature waterfalls, stone votive lamps, and grotesquely trained trees, dwarfed by some strange process to accord with the minuteness of their surroundings.

Whilst we are observing all these things, and the now blossomless wisterias in their belated garb of light green, our mousmé returns, staggering along with two huge iron candlesticks three feet high, one in each hand, which are to light us at our feast. With great exactitude, she sticks two wax candles upon their respective spikes, and lights them; and then vanishes, like the genie of the lamp, to carry out further bidding.

Although the garden and tea-house were so full of patrons, we had not long to wait for our refreshments. Our mousmé knew that I was English—not, of, course, a difficult matter; and to be English spells generosity in Japanese eyes in the matter of sen for her own little pocket. So we were waited on quickly.

In a few minutes we seemed positively surrounded by tiny dishes and plates.

As an Irish gentleman who came to Japan for three months, and made my acquaintance, once said, "Everything relating to meals is so singularly numerous."

This exactly puts it.

We had ordered a simple enough meal, in all conscience, and yet we were literally surrounded by it.

Mousmé sipped her light-coloured tea, which was suffused with cherry blossoms, with the air of a princess, and behaved as a great lady. At any rate the attendant mousmé should clearly understand that she was not like the party of geishas over there in the brilliantly lighted pagoda near the balcony, who were entertaining and being entertained by some of the gilded youths of Nagasaki.

"What a noise they make!" exclaims Mousmé with a smile of pitying disgust. "Their laugh is as hollow as a drum, and they sing because they must. They will be with some one else to-morrow night, and the next, and the next. While," and the expression of Mousmé's face changes and grows very soft and tender, "I have always you."

"Yes, always me," I answer, taking her hand that she has rested on my knee whilst talking.

Chapter VII

Next morning I awoke early, roused by the twittering of grass sparrows and the weakened croak of a frog, hoarse from its vocal efforts of the night.

It was New Year's day, and the sun was streaming through the open windows. Mousmé had already crept from her white mattress beneath the smoke-blue mosquito curtains, and was doubtless sunning herself, after a hasty toilet, in the wonderful garden which we had fashioned out of the rocks and red-brown soil.

I stretched sleepily, and wondered vaguely what they were doing in England, and whether my estimable, though trying, sister Lou (fashionable to her finger-tips) had cajoled my unfortunate brother-in-law into changing her last year's set of furs for "something a little more the thing, don't you know, Stanmere."

Mousmé requires no furs. Her wants are few. A piece of silk with wonderful patterns over it—birds which seem to fly, irises whose vivid tints almost make unaccustomed eyes ache, and chrysanthemums which one could swear nod upon their slender, almost leafless stalks—which she fashions into a robe of delight. A few jade and lacquer pins for her wonderful jet-black hair. Some new tabi. Long white digitated stockings reaching above her dimpled knees. A sash to make her girl acquaintances and married brother's wife jealous. And so you have the costume in which she is prepared to receive her visitors and to glide with a soothing shish-shish over the white matting of the floor and through the comically narrow passages.

The mail arrived yesterday week, and down at Kotmasu's office I found Lou's usual parcel of New Year's gifts. For me there were several new novels—the pictures in which will cause Mousmé to wonder and open her almond eyes wide, with the little trick of quivering the lids which she has—some papers, tobacco—five pounds of it in a sealed tin (a good soul is Stanmere)—a shaving tidy worked by Irene in some mysterious stitch which seems to have come into fashion since I scorned crewel-work anti-macassars with lace frills that hung on the back buttons of one's coat, turning one at afternoon tea into an object of interest and amusement.

For Mousmé there was a Paris hat (Lou will never, I fear, realise that Paris fashions have as yet little interest for Nagasaki belles), in which Mousmé's piquant face would be smothered and turned to no account, a silk tea-gown which she will wear with the dignity becoming five feet one inch and a half of really married Japanese womanhood.

There was also something more.

My present, which I have had sent out from the Compagnie des Fondants Parisiens—a huge box of the best confectionery that money could buy. I knew that Mousmé would like this better than anything else, and that for the time the native teriyaki and such-like sugar-coated joys would be nowhere.

All the presents are in the little room I use as a study—a room into which Mousmé creeps with awe. It is (to her untutored mind) so full of books and mysterious writings.

I had risen and was gazing out over the harbour, which lay below me veiled in a gauze-like, opalescent haze, when the farther paper-panelled door was slid softly back in its groove, and Mousmé entered.

A quaint little figure with the flush of dawn transferred to her porcelain cheeks and eyes bright with the early morning air of the scented garden; her elaborate coiffure, with its many pins, a striking contrast to the négligée of her plum-coloured kimono with its sprays of bamboo in gold thread. Against her bare little throat and dimpled shoulders she pressed a wealth of iris and lotus blooms and tender green shoots of the slenderest bamboo, her face peeping out elfish and smiling from the midst.

"These are for you, Cy-reel," she said, laughing and casting the brilliant blossoms on to the floor in a patch of sunlight at my feet. "Now den what have you for me?"

It is difficult to resist Mousmé when she pulls one's face down to her own smiling one, and throws slender but wonderfully tenacious little arms round one's neck.

Mousmé, since she married, has lost some of the shyness for the "velly much rich Englishman" who had so strange a fancy as to marry her right away, and in its place has come the knowledge of certain privileges of her sex (for she knows little as yet of the "advanced" woman), and she exacts them with a pretty persistence which I find charming.

We went along the passage to the room in which are all the presents. They have been taken out of their case, and piled with masculine breadth of effect upon two low lacquer-and-bamboo settees in a corner near one of the windows.

"Oh! Oh!" exclaimed Mousmé, and then she fell down before this wonderful collection of gifts, her tiny hands fluttering over them like those of a child uncertain which thing to touch first.

Irene's shaving tidy, the tin of tobacco sent by Stanmere, Lou's gift of books—all these things are brushed aside, and the wonderful pale blue tea-gown is at last taken up. It is absurdly long for her, of course, and as she slipped into it she laughed softly at the comical figure she presented.

"It is velly nice, I like it. But it must be cut off. You cannot come near me with all this on the floor."

She glided once or twice across the room, like a big-winged moth, with the soft sound of silk frou-frou on the matting, and then the gown was laid aside, so that she might more easily find the other presents.

Then the box of fondants was discovered. What rapture! Smiles stole over her face. Her little fingers trembled when she at last made up her mind to undo the satin ribbon, which, crossing from corner to corner, is tied in a great bow in the centre of the lid. There are wonderful sweets of all sorts, things which Mousmé almost fears to taste, and which when once tasted encourage her to further depredations and experiments.

"Mousmé, you'll be ill."

"No, Cy-reel, not nearly so sweet and ill-producing as teriyaki."

I laughed at the gentle sophistry and suggested that we should go to breakfast.

After the meal a huge bullock-cart came along the road which runs at the foot of our sloping garden. It is laden with New Year's gifts to tempt those who have put off the inevitable spending of sen and yen till the last possible moment.

Mousmé drew me along the garden path, past the iris pond, in the shade of which gold-fish are keeping New Year's day on a fly-and-mosquito diet, to the side of the cart. The proprietors in new suits are explaining the merits of their wares, which are cheapened enormously as at Western "sale" times. A light air stirred the paper lanterns with which the cart was decked.

One represented a huge gold-fish with a gold and vermilion body and fins boldly sketched in black. It took Mousmé's fancy. We purchased it, and earned the absurdly exaggerated thanks of the smiling vendors, knowing the while that we did not require it, and that it would be placed with a score of others, hung on their slight bamboo rods, in the cupboard at the end of the passage.

Some night, perhaps, unless another lantern comes more easily to hand, we might take it out to guide us on our way down to the chaya at which the best geishas dance.

During the whole of the morning we were expectant. Before sunset many of Mousmé's numerous relations will have called to wish us New Year joys: and my respected, if too effusive, mother-in-law will have once more asked me if I am satisfied with her daughter.

She even yet seems to think that her daughter is on approval, and liable at any time to be returned with liquidated damages in the form of an extra handsome kimono from Nara-Ya's famous store on the Bund. Everyone calls on everyone, and after mid-day we are not long left without visitors.

Kotmasu turned up in good time. He brought Mousmé the tiny dog she has been longing for. A charming present, which she will almost want to wear round her neck with a chain, lest it be lost.

It was only when our little home almost trembled and our garden seemed to swarm with the incursion of Mousmé's relatives that I realised how thoroughly I was married. By the time the sun had commenced its downward flight into the sea behind the hills, many had arrived, and little moon-faced Aki had taken the usual and seemingly inevitable plunge into the water-lily pond in search of the sprites who are supposed to dwell therein.

These obsequious relatives by marriage amuse me immensely. They all take so much au sérieux. But how truly polite they all are. Even the sampanman (a cousin of whom Mousmé is not quite sure) is a polished gentleman, and the new suit with which he has managed to start the year, with the manners thrown in, gave him quite a distinguished air. I noticed that the box of sweets was reserved by Mousmé for those who were drinking tea, surrounded by many plates and cups—the favoured few, mostly girl friends.

If only I might have believed the charming prevarications of my relatives, how beautiful everything belonging to me must have been.

At length the last of them disappeared down the road. And the paper lanterns, whose dull white surfaces challenge the moon swinging in the sky above the amethyst hills, swung round the corner. Mousmé waved her hand sympathetically, and then we sat down together on the veranda to watch the last hours of a New Year's Day glide into the aeons of the past.

One day is so very much like another to me in this strange land, where I have the lightest of business duties to perform, few friends other than Kotmasu, and no great desire to gain any more, though I find the natives I know vastly more interesting than the few English who are settled more or less permanently in Nagasaki for business or other purposes.

Everything has a certain charm—Mousmé always—but four long years have robbed my surroundings of that subtlest of all interests, novelty. I am eager to test my experiment, which is answering here so admirably, with a new environment.

"Mousmé in Bond Street." Kotmasu's phrase haunts me with a sinister purpose, but I am not to be daunted easily, for I have my own opinions. Have I not? I ask myself.

I remember the Frenchman who, with some delicacy, sums up the question of marriage in every clime where any ceremony is attached to the rite: "Given a woman and one possesses the possibility of great happiness—or its exact antithesis," and I am thankful that my experiment so far has resulted well.

Mousmé is neither the serpent nor the eel of another French writer's experience, but is always fresh, always charming. She is a graduate in the art of pleasing. She knows nothing further of astronomy than to suspect that the stars are really big diamonds, nor of mathematics than what generally enables her to make a good bargain for an obi, dress or hairpin. Hers are entirely applied mathematics, and of the simplest kind. All this ignorance is very stupid, no doubt, to you. I can well imagine the smile of the Girton girl or "superior person" which will reward my confession of Mousmé's ignorance, but then you are at a disadvantage—in short, you do not know Mousmé as I do. She has lately taken to writing me love-letters whilst I am away down in the town, and when she is tired of trying to read what is printed underneath the pictures in the papers and magazines—queer narrow little strips of letters, folded ever so many times, which she places in her prettiest envelopes, and lays upon my writing-desk; then hides behind a paper screen, or in the next room, to watch me unobserved whilst I read them.

Of course, she could tell me all that they contain, and often does; but Mousmé is quite a child in some things—the blending of childishness with womanhood, which is one of her most delightful traits.

There are such quaint turns of expression in these rice-paper billets-doux, which by turns bring smiles and tears into my eyes, such naïve confessions, such strange lapses into her limited vocabulary of English words.

To-day there is one of those notes on my writing-table, in a shrimp-pink envelope, on which is depicted a dainty little geisha dancing in one corner. There is a rather strong air—I cannot call it a wind, or even breeze—stirring; and Mousmé, fearful lest the treasury of her love should be blown away, has weighed it down with the bronze frog I use for a paper-weight, which she made me buy as an ornament (!) for my table the other day.

I take the little letter up, of course, with the knowledge that Mousmé's eye is upon me from some near retreat, from which she can steal forth silently to kiss me, English fashion; or startle me with some sudden noise, in imitation of the mice which scamper about in the basement at night, or with a mimicry of the strange han! han! of the vultures which whirl, screaming hoarsely and as if in complaint, over the water of the harbour below.

Mousmé comes out softly from her hiding-place behind the turquoise-blue paper screen in the corner, unaware that two tell-tale glasses, her big one (which she soon made me purchase for her) and my little one, have from their juxtaposition long ago betrayed to me the secret of her whereabouts.

Two soft white arms, bare to the elbows, encircle my neck suddenly from behind; a pretty, piquant face appears over my left shoulder, and—well, after a time, when we stand up and look at each other, there is a peal of gay, spontaneous laughter. And, behold! there is a tell-tale patch of white upon my cheek and coat where her face has rested.

It is several days since we have been anywhere—that is, further afield than a flying visit to my mother-in-law down the hill—and to-night we are going to the fête at the great temple away up the hillside. I have been to such before, but Mousmé is crazy to go with her real husband; and as there is certainly no valid objection to urge against her desire, we are going.

Mousmé puts the little shrimp-coloured love-letter in a box on top of the numerous others she has written me during our three months of married life, and then we sit down to a dinner of the usual perplexing dishes.

We talk gaily enough in Japanese, Mousmé describing to me all the delights she is anticipating from the proposed excursion, and telling me all that has occurred during my two hours' absence.

What a charming little vis-a-vis she proves as we, seated on our squares of spotless matting, pretend to make a good meal off impossible dishes, as to the constituents of which, even now, after some years of experience, I am frequently in mysterious doubt! Oka, our cook, is of an inventive turn of mind, and to-day he serves on the tiny blue plates wee potatoes à la marrons glacés, and cherries in vinegar! But Mousmé pronounces them a success, and insists on leaning across the elaborate square of magenta silk worked with white cranes fishing, which she has instituted as a tribute to European ideas of a table-cloth, to put the larger of the cherries in my mouth on the end of a chop-stick. All this is very frivolous, doubtless; but very charming. To be anything but gay with such make-believe surroundings, and Mousmé sitting opposite playful and smiling, would be out of place. I assert this to myself whenever the thought of Lou crosses my mind. I am compelled to do so to lay the ghost of Lou's outraged sense of propriety, for, truth to tell, she is very proper over some things, a somewhat hide-bound devotee of society etiquette with the responsibilities of a rapidly upgrowing daughter.

What a child Mousmé is! And yet there is an indefinable charm inseparable from womanhood about her. She was pouting just now because the camellia she had stuck in the front of her gown had fallen in a shower of scarlet petals into a tiny cup of tea on her knees. Now she is smiling again, and giving herself a lesson in English.

"Cy-reel! Cy-reel!" She always seems to practise this first; and then, "I luv yew. I luv yew velly much." This over and over again, till we both burst out laughing, and the scene ends in the usual way.

At present our life is a dainty comédie à deux, and is nothing approaching the farce with its underlying tragic note which timorous Kotmasu feared and predicted.

Soon after sunset we start out—Mousmé and I—to make our way to the temple. The moon swims up rapidly into the cloud-clear vault of heaven, and floods our scented garden with a pure silver radiance. We have our paper lanterns all the same, although in competition with the strong white moonbeams they look almost trumpery.

Our garden, with its narrow paths and tangled vegetation, is full of exquisite perfumes released by the blossoming flowers, scents wafted under one's nostrils by the faintest breath of air, which causes the full-blown tea-roses to shiver and then shatter in a hail of falling petals.

As we turn the corner of the path near the largest of our several fountains, we look back (as we always do) at our home. The door-panels of the rooms leading on to the verandah are open, and I can see right into our bed-chamber. On its bracket a little lamp is burning, and near it Mousmé has placed a tiny image of Buddha— an ivory god with a fixed smile. She does not pray to it now, however. I am vaguely conscious that I have ousted the ivory Buddha from its temple. Why Mousmé keeps it there I have been as yet unable to discover. How strange it seems to leave the whole side of one's house open after dark! Ere we step out on to the road through the bamboo wicket with its quaintly chased brass hinges, I take one more look back, and see Oka's wife with her funny little squat figure pass along the verandah on her way to tidy the rooms.

Mousmé is charmingly dressed to-night in a peach-coloured silk gown, so stiff and rich, and an amber-yellow sash. Her hair is done into a marvellous butterfly, and her head is full of half a score of the most handsome of her many pins. The moonlight gives a silver sheen to her ebon locks; and did I not know how black they are, I might have a chill come to my heart because of Mousmé's getting grey.

We make our way as rapidly as we can down into the town.

Long before we arrive at the commencement of the town proper we are made aware that the fête is in full swing by the sounds of gaiety, the blaze of lanterns which is reflected above the town as if there were a conflagration, and the softened, confused roar of the thronging multitudes in the streets.

We reach the end of the street at last, and Mousmé is almost torn from my arm by the crowd by which we are immediately absorbed.

Every one is gay and good-humoured. I tread upon some one's heels, but he only smiles, and assures me that my "honourable feet" have not hurt his humble heel. My toes are trodden on in turn, Mousmé laughs, and even I, the injured party, do not remonstrate. Indeed, I almost say, "Gomen navai," as though I were the offender and do murmur politely—"It is no matter"—that is all I reply to the polite speech with which the offender asks pardon.

Mousmé is used to this, and she pilots me amid this bewildering blaze of ambulatory lanterns, swaying recklessly on the ends of their quivering sticks.

The moving crowds of women and girls diffuse a subtle perfume from the flowers they wear in their dresses and hair. Mousmés in the brilliant colours of their gayest holiday attire jostle one another good-humouredly—laughing, thoughtless little souls. The men are seemingly suffering from a bad attack of "European fever," as is indicated by the frequent presence of the top-hat or "bowler" above their amiable though unbeautiful faces, and the occasional presence of trousers beneath their skirt-like robes.

Alas! just as we near the temple, the pressure of the throng drives us into the proximity of my mother-in-law, and little Aki, who is carrying high above his queer shaven head, with its one tuft of hair or rather fringe—which is like nothing so much as the traditional chimney-sweep's circular broom—a lantern, like the banner in "Excelsior," "with a strange device"—a most quaintly hideous imp.

Mother-in-law is too busy protecting one of my "handsome presents," a ruby-coloured silken obi, from contamination with the crowd, to notice us. But I quickly perceive that Aki's narrow slots of eyes have spied us out, for the imp-like lantern sways violently upon its stick as he pushes his way through the dense crowd towards us.

We are so hedged in that escape is impossible even if we wished; but Mousmé has a penchant for this queer little brother with his intelligent monkey-face and ever-present smile.

She, too, has caught sight of the struggling Aki, who at times seems swallowed up in the crowd, as though never to reappear. But he does. And we can see him working an eel-like course towards the fluttering banner under which he doubtless noticed we were standing.

He reaches us at last, and advertises the fact by unconsciously swinging his imp lantern into my face.

Mousmé bursts out laughing, and so do I—merriment is so infectious; and in a moment the people near us are laughing too.

Aki is delighted, and seizes hold of a hand of mine and one of Mousmé's, and we advance along the street a little further.

The shops we pass are simply blazing with lights. They have stall-like extensions, encroaching upon the roadway, all of them piled up with astonishing sweetmeats of brilliant hues, toys, flowers, and hideously grotesque masks.

Aki is so attracted by the latter that we make scarcely any progress. Mousmé, who is getting impatient, makes a brilliant suggestion.

"Cy-reel, buy Aki a mask. He will never cease gazing at them or come along if you don't. And we shall never reach the temple. No one can see my obi and dress here."

I laugh quietly to myself at this last remark. The woman had popped out unwittingly.

I buy my little brother-in-law a most monstrous head. He is in raptures, and Mousmé and I are in convulsions of laughter at the hideous god into which little Aki is at once transformed. We get on famously now, till his acquisitive eyes light upon a pile of crystal trumpets.

"Ah!" exclaims Mousmé, as she sees him pause, "he must have one."

It is obvious that queer little Aki's heart is set upon possessing one of these weirdly articulate instruments, so another quarter of a yen changes hands, and Aki adds his quota to the unearthly, gobbling sounds which dozens of these strange instruments produce, blown by other equally lusty-lunged boys.

The houses we pass by are all thrown open, and decorated exquisitely with flowers and foliage. It is a scene of fairy-like beauty, and Mousmé at my side, upon whom I have to look down to admire, is a fairy.

She is getting tired; Aki is dragging on her arm, and I am glad when the climb up is done, and we are at last at the bottom of the first flight of the temple steps.

Below us once more, as from our verandah (only from a different and almost opposite point) we see the town and the land-locked bay flooded in a silver haze of moonlight, which fails, however, to make the crimson and golden reflection from the thousands of lanterns less apparent.

The scene is like nothing that can be imagined in beauty, and all around us appears to be enveloped in a veil of impalpable light.

We are close to the portico of the temple, and we pass underneath it and enter the courtyard, carried onward by the pressure of the multitude from behind.

We pass two enormous white-and-blue porcelain lanterns with encircling serpents of mythological type, and then we are in fairyland again.

Mousmé heaves a little sigh of delight; her colour is deepened by the crimson of excitement, and her eyes are dancing like fire-flies. Aki is lost, and we forget all about him. He will be all right. There are scores of other children straying about, and no one seems to take any notice. Besides, they mostly wear masks, and blow intermittently upon crystal horns, the noise of which reminds me of the irate gobble-gobble of turkeys engaged in a farmyard fracas.

"Cy-reel, is England like this?" Mousmé asks in an excited whisper.

"No," I am forced to admit, though foreseeing the inevitable rejoinder.

"Then I don't think I shall like England," says Mousmé the child.

"We shall see."

We make our way to the terrace, bordered by tea-houses, now thronged by the beauties and golden youths of Nagasaki and the country round. At every turn we seem to meet some acquaintance of Mousmé's, who keeps up a continuous series of bows and nods and smiles.

The grove of giant camellias, camphor-wood trees, and cryptomerias stretch out like a vast roof, the camellias covered with a wealth of blood-red blossoms which, falling in continuous showers in the vibrating air, form a crimson carpet under the feet. Even the dark recesses are luminous with the flood of light which streams from the lanterns and brilliantly illuminated interiors of the tea-houses. We find seats at last.

In an instant a mousmé with huge pins in her hair, a humble smile, and gaily rouged and whitened cheeks, brings us tiny cups of tea.

Beyond and below us we can hear noises which tell of the presence of side-shows, wrestlers, mountebanks; and the roar of approving audiences makes Mousmé hasten to drink her tea and eat her beans in sugar with the greatest possible speed.

When she has finished, we make our way along a terrace and take up our position to form a part of the audience outside a miniature theatre.

There is not much to see. What there is would scarcely amuse any one less unsophisticated in the Thespian art than the Japanese. It is something like a shadow-show. Only the horrible puppets which appear and go through almost incomprehensible antics are realities, which, in truly terrifying masks, cause Mousmé what are known as delightful "creeps," and send her hand clutching at my arm. The noises from an orchestra of four or five which accompany the doings of the characters, some of which are a mixture of man and beast, ghoul-like and given to sudden and unlooked-for appearances and disappearances, are weird and disquieting; of harmony the musicians know nothing. Their colour tones are all blues, greens, grays, and bilious yellows; their merits, that they are in accord with the impressions of the puppets.

We remain watching these human puppets for some time, surrounded by a dense crowd craning their necks, and on tip-toe as each new shadow appears upon the scene. Some of the antics of these shadow-like forms are so monstrous that I begin to think that Mousmé is getting really frightened, and so I propose moving on to where some clever tumblers, contortionists and conjurers are to be seen.

"No," says Mousmé, "let us go home."

Then, seeing I do not quite understand her desire, she explains with charming naïveté that she is afraid of bad dreams.

How queer, little Mousmé! and how childlike, to be sure!

Mousmé's words have made me notice that the crowd is lessening in density, and the lanterns are going out. Or is it they are paling before the coming dawn?

I look into the face of Mousmé, and then into the faces of the people near us. Yes, that is it. The moon is gone down into the sea, and the sun will be climbing up the first steps of another day's journey ere we arrive home.

We leave the terrace, with its lingering crowds of tired-faced holiday-makers, and fading light of lanterns and tea-houses, and by a short cut gain a mountain-path leading close home.

The sound of the trumpets is less and less distinct, and that of the ever-chirping cicalas more so, as we wend our way—Mousmé and I—along the narrow, rough, unpaved path in the rapidly growing dawn of a Japanese morning.

Below us to the left lies the town as yet indistinct in the slowly increasing light, a mysterious mass of shadows and projections which mark the places of streets and roofs of houses. Here and there twinkle yellowish red points of light which grow dimmer each moment in the quickening dawn. The harbour stretches a mist-obscured expanse, with gaps here and there like chrysoprases laid in cotton wool. Soon the shipping will become visible, and the mist roll off the face of the tranquil water, like a gauze curtain lifted by unseen hands.

The path runs between fields of flowers, and is edged with dewy grass. The perfume of the blossoms and the keen freshness of the morning air arouse Mousmé's almost slumbering senses. Through the indescribable fragrance and glamour of an Eastern dawn we wend our way homewards slowly and with tired feet.

The women, in blue cotton garments, are already coming up to work in the fields. Good-looking children accompanying them chase each other across the dew-spangled grass, trampling under foot flowers which would have graced a palace.

At last we have walked up the little garden path, slippery now with the morning exhalations. Indoors all are asleep. Everywhere is quiet.

But no matter. When Mousmé has drowsily mounted the verandah steps we have only to enter our little house, which looks so lonely and mysterious at this early hour, by pushing aside one of those sliding paper panels; to cross the creaking floor covered with spotlessly clean matting; and then fall asleep in two minutes on the soft, mosquito-guarded mattress, lulled, if we need a lullaby, by Oka's muffled snores down below.

Chapter VIII

It is nearly a month since our night of pleasure at the temple fête of the thousands of lanterns, and I have been in terrible trouble.

Something has happened to Mousmé, and till that catastrophe—to me it seemed nothing less—I never realized what she was to me.

It was so sudden.

I had left her in the morning, bright as the sunshine which forced its way through the bamboo and paper shoji, and, filtering thus, fell in golden, thread-like rays like spun silk upon the floor. The last I saw of her was a tiny figure upon the balcony as I turned the corner of the road, blowing kisses to me with one hand, and waving a huge bunch of crimson lotus in the other, flowers we had just gathered together in the sun-bathed garden.

And in three or four hours all this was altered, obliterated.

I climbed up from the town leisurely, taking the shady side of the road, and availing myself to the full of every shadow cast by the trees or by the queer old villas with their mossy roofs and eccentric architecture. If I had but known, how my steps would have hastened!

Arrived at the wicket, I cannot see even a flutter of Mousmé's dress to-day. She is usually awaiting my return in the shady corner of the verandah with her samisen, or with a pile of books at her side, from which she has been trying to spell out the words in big print.

I walk up the path, which is flower-bordered, and alive with bees whose humming sounds are like the deeper notes of an Aeolian harp, and across the garden where dragon-flies flit, iridescent shuttles weaving their colours, blue, green and yellow, into the sunlit air, darting between the little ponds in which gold-fish hide from the sunlight beneath the tranquil floating lotus-leaves.

I enter the house. Everything is strangely still.

There is no one in the room in which we usually sit. The blue-and-white vases of Arita porcelain are filled with lotus-blooms, dainty, fantastic in their arrangement, with spiked grasses and sedges. A tiny vase of bronze stands upon my writing-table. As usual, dear little Mousmé has placed in it the finest blossoms, and in their rose-hued cups I fancy some of her kisses may lurk. Her shoes are standing in a patch of sunlight on the floor. "She cannot have gone out, then," I say to myself. "It is evident that she is not down at mother-in-law's."

Where is she?

I push back one of the panels to enter the next room. Perhaps she is there.

The room is so dark that I can scarcely see across it; but in the dimness I can just discern a something stretched upon the floor.

I step hastily forward.

Yes, it is Mousmé lying there, with her face, upturned, looking a white, featureless oval in the gloom, her gown elongating her slender figure, and her huge sleeves of blue flowered silk with orange linings spread out like the maimed wings of a brilliant, long-bodied moth.

I stoop down.

Is she asleep? No, but she is terribly still. Is it a coquettish ruse on her part, and will she open her eyes in a minute or two, and burst out laughing in my face, and then pull it down for a shower of kisses from her rosebud mouth?

Half expecting this, I wait an instant, and feel as if I were kneeling beside my own grave. But the fantastic little figure I love so well gives no sign of movement. My alarm increases. I get up, hastily push back one of the sliding paper panels, and let in a flood of sunlight from the garden.

It streams full on Mousmé's face; it searches out the gold threads in the embroidery of her gown; it tells me in an instant that there is something seriously wrong.

There are no bells in this strange little house of mine, so I beat upon the floor with my heel to summon Oka or his wife.

I wait anxiously, kneeling beside silent little Mousmé. Each second seems to extend itself into an hour. How long it seems— that minute or two ere I can hear some one ascending the rickety stairs from the basement. It is Oka's wife who enters, her eyes still but half unfastened from an interrupted siesta.

She comes forward to where I am kneeling beside Mousmé.

Unlike women of her class in England, Oka's wife is laconic.

"Fever," she says, on catching sight of Mousmé's face. "Send for the doctor very quick!" She is evidently waiting for me to give my assent to her suggestion, so I nod my head, and she goes away softly across the room.

A few minutes later I hear one of her numerous progeny go away down the path at a run, and I know the doctor has been sent for.

Mousmé remains unconscious all the time that we are getting her partially undressed and on to the mattress.

Am I to lose her?

The bare thought drives the blood away from my heart. I know what Kotmasu would say, for he still disbelieves, or at least pretends to disbelieve, in my marriage.

"There are velly plenty more mousmés."

"Yes, very well," something inside my mind replies, "but only one Mousmé."

Whilst we wait the coming of Han Sen, the doctor, I am driven almost frantic by the noises which one can never shut out of a Japanese house. The droning hum of the bees at work on the roses outside, the unceasing chirruping whirr of the cicalas, all the sounds of a garden in summer-time, are magnified tenfold because I fear that Mousmé will be disturbed.

She uncloses her eyes once when the doctor's steps are heard coming up the garden-path. But she says nothing, and only takes my large brown hand in her small one.

I have not much faith in the doctor. His phials are so finikin and toy-like, and I have heard something, too, about their drugs, and my memory of their fantastic and extraordinary nature does not tend to reassure me.

He is a little, oldish man with gimlet eyes in a face full of wrinkles, which seem to serve no other purpose than to disguise his emotions if he has any. He treads softly across the matting floor, with Oka's wife hovering, anxious-faced, in the rear.

"Madame the most honourable lady has been unwell some time?" he inquires in a high-pitched key, with an insinuating inflection on the first word, which many people annoy me with when referring to Mousmé.

"No."

"No!" and his eyebrows depart upward from overhanging his narrow, beady black eyes.

"Her illness dates but from an hour or two ago."

"Ah, then she will get better, most honourable English Mister," is the reply. And then, whilst I am explaining matters, the doctor's yellow fingers, with their wrinkled, dried-parchment skin, are busy compounding something which smells abominably, and in the efficacy of which I feel I have no faith, notwithstanding his reiterated assurance that "the most honourable madame" will speedily recover.

When he has finished mixing the medicine in the little jar-like cup Oka's wife has brought him, he examines his patient very carefully with a pair of spectacles thrust up on his forehead, holding Mousmé's hand and counting the pulse-beats, lifting her eyelids and staring into her unseeing eyes, talking all the while in the high-pitched, squeaky tone which reminds me of the old man who sits at the corner of Nisson Street and writes the illiterate mousmés' love-letters, putting in all sorts of dreadful things in response to the usual, "You know what to say," of his unimaginative clients.

When Dr. Han Sen has finished the examination, and has listened with a stethoscope of native manufacture to the beating of Mousmé's heart, to the bird-like fluttering of which I am so used in the wakeful stillness of the night, he rises to go.

Shall he come to see the most honourable lady to-morrow?

A vague idea formulates itself as I look into his unintelligent, vacuous face.

"No, I will send if I want your services," I hastily explain.

"No?" There is a look of almost professional regret on the wizened face. Do I know my most honourable madame is ill, very ill?

"Yes! I know. I will send if I require the most honourable Dr. Han Sen."

Then he goes out down the path, no doubt mystified at my eccentric conduct.

What a fool I was not to have thought of this before!

As soon as Dr. Han Sen has had time to get clear of the garden, I hasten off down into Nagasaki, leaving Mousmé, who is evidently sleeping now, in charge of Oka's wife.

I am going to get the European doctor of the mail-boat to come and see her.

"Why did not I think of this before?" I ask myself as I hasten over the roughly paved roadway down the hillside towards the harbour. Ah! why, indeed, not?

Mousmé was very ill, and at one time I watched beside her day and night, fearing every hour, nay, almost every moment, lest the frail thread of life should be snapped, and the sun of my happiness go down with that of her life.

My friend M'Phail, the cheery doctor of the mail-boat, was most untiring in his attendance; and at last I think professional interest in the case was replaced by a deep and friendly one. Oka's wife, who has seen so many cases of fever, and so many lives allowed to slip through the native practitioners' fingers, is unceasing in her praises of the ship's doctor, whose skill and resourcefulness seem to her simple mind nothing short of miraculous. Indeed, she almost forgets to give the family god, before whose impassive figure a light has been kept burning night and day during her mistress's illness, any credit for Mousmé's wonderful recovery.

However, when she remembers it, she in penitence places additional offerings of fruit and flowers on the little shelf on which the image stands, and when I go down to give some order to Oka, I see her prostrated, in the comparative gloom of their basement bed-chamber, pouring out her supplications, whilst the scent of burnt incense pervades the house more than ever.

When she hears me she comes out, half fearing lest I should treat her orisons with ridicule.

"Him hear," she says, pointing and nodding in the direction where the idol sits solemnly, in a halo of yellow light from the little earthen-ware lamp. "Missus"—she has mastered the word, and uses it with infinite care—"velly much better."

"Yes," I reply.

And who knows, Oka's wife, perhaps your prayers offered in good faith have reached ears that are not deaf, and have brought an answer from "the God of the English sir," I say to myself.

Chapter IX

Mousmé is better.

At last, after weary and anxious days of waiting and watching, the crisis is past. From that mysterious land, whose borders so often touch ours in sleep and illness, in which Mousmé had almost set foot, my little wife has returned. A frail ghost of her former bright self. One who looks as though she had seen visions.

She seems more fairy-like than ever, sitting out under the verandah, wrapped up in an elaborate dressing-gown of silver-grey silk with a delicate rose-pink lining. She doesn't look a whit older—Japanese women never appear so till they are quite old—only more like some toy woman taken bodily from off a screen or jar decorated by an artist drawing his inspiration from models of the highest types.

There seems something almost unreal in the slight figure in its quaint Eastern dress, and the dainty ways that are returning to her one by one with the strength which comes back so slowly.

Oka's wife is delighted. She is very fond of the little mistress, who is so gay and childlike and amiable. I shall be sorry when the time comes for us to leave old Oka, with his ugly, amiable, yellow face, and his wife, who is, as are many of the lower-class women, really more than passably good-looking, though verging upon forty.

We sit out almost all day long; and when I am obliged to leave Mousmé to attend to business in the town, Oka's wife sits within call, and Mousmé looks at the pictures in the illustrated papers and magazines Lou has from time to time sent me; or pores over a tattered copy of a rudimentary English spelling-book and grammar combined, which Chen Yo, the publisher of the principal paper, put aside for me as a great curiosity which he had bought one day.

Mousmé is learning English well. Her accent is still peculiar, of course, though her vocabulary is greatly extended. I talk to her as much as I can, for soon English will be the only language she will hear.

These are ever-to-be-remembered days, spent in my Japanese home overlooking the wonderful garden, full of brilliance of flower, earth, life and sky. I smoke, and Mousmé plays her guitar; and she sings in a voice into which love and patience have translated greater harmony and sweetness than any other woman's voice that I have heard during the last four years—

"What shall I sing to thee, my love?

In the garden where the moonbeams play,

And pipe the nightingale and dove,

And plash the fountain's silver spray.

"What shall I bring to thee, my own?

Visions of heaven's mansions fair;

Never had king a truer throne

Than my heart's casket rich and rare."

"Sing on, little Mousmé; there are other verses of your little love-song," I say.

But she is tired, and, unconsciously like a European prima donna, only sings the last two lines over again—

"Never had king a truer throne

Than my heart's casket rich and rare."

"True, Mousmé, true," I say, half to myself, as the song loses itself in the air. But she catches the words, and smiles.

The wet season is coming on, alas! before I can leave, and our evenings beneath the verandah will be less frequent. It is not nearly so pleasant indoors, but the damp air is bad for Mousmé. So we play Japanese draughts, and talk of England.

Sometimes Kotmasu comes in. He is convinced at last of the bona-fides of my marriage, and is as profuse in his apologies for ever having doubted the success of my experiment, as he was with his lugubrious predictions that it would never succeed.

We are always glad to see him; for since Mousmé's illness I have been into the tea-houses, and even the town itself, very little. We hear gossip from my queer mother-in-law, but it is usually only a chronique scandaleuse of the doings of the geishas, of her friends, and last, though by no means least, of her enemies, half of whom I do not even know by name.

Kotmasu, on the other hand, has always some scrap of more or less reliable European news, which, if it does nothing else, serves as a peg on which to hang a reminiscence, or an echo to awaken old memories of Western men and things.

The evenings we spend together are far from being uninteresting; and Mousmé, who has picked up the art of conversation wonderfully, is delighted to intrude her quaint ideas upon us. She is burning with curiosity concerning the strange country called England, which Kotmasu, willing enough to shine even in the eyes of a married woman, and she my wife, pretends he knows so well.

He is really very funny in his descriptions sometimes. In a sense they are fairly correct; but they are, just like all Japanese pictures, lacking in the most elementary perspective. It is not because his perceptive faculties are lacking, but only that they follow the national groove, the worship of the minute to the exclusion of broader effects.

Mousmé, no doubt with a desire to be in the possession of two opinions, addresses a multitude of questions to him when, as is the case to-night, he is spending the evening with us.

"What do the women wear? How do they dress? Are their obis as handsome as mine?" and so on.

Kotmasu endeavors to describe the attire of my fellow-countrymen, blundering magnificently over its hidden intricacies.

"It is dull, very dull indeed," he explains, with an apologetic glance in my direction, as if fearful that I should seek to upset his statement. "There are no colours worn—at least," he hastens to add, with another glance over in my direction through the tiny cloud of bluish-grey smoke his absurd tobacco-pipe permits him to eject, "not colours like ours. Not like you are wearing, Mousmé."

I laugh to myself, partially at the perplexed expression on Mousmé's face, and partially at the idea of her promenading in England in all the glory of a canary-coloured obi, plum-coloured gown embroidered in gold thread, and a bifurcated garment of ivory satin.

"The women wear no obis," continues Kotmasu, complacently.

"No obis!" ejaculates Mousmé, evidently incredulous.

"No. Sometimes the children do."

"It is velly stlange," says Mousmé, "and they not look velly large here. See!" she continues, placing her tiny hands as though to span her waist. "What do they wear then?"

Kotmasu is launched forthwith into a veritable catalogue. The garments comprised in which must be individually explained for Mousmé's enlightenment. Kotmasu, plunging innocently into the sea of impropriety, at last succeeds in satisfying her curiosity.

As we rise and step out upon the verandah to get a breath of cooler air, she comes close to me, and taking my hand in her pretty I-wish-to-be-protected way, whispers in Japanese, "How strange it will be! Cy-reel, I am a little frightened; I feel like the other night when I was awoke by the nidzoumi scampering across the floor, and squeak, squeaking in the walls."

Mousmé is like her Western sisters in her fear of mice.

"But I shall be there, Mousmé," I reply, as she squeezes my hand.

"Yes, Cy-reel;" then with a coquettish smile, which I can see ere we pass out into the gloom of the verandah, "perhaps, perhaps it may be all right."

It had been raining. Such torrents of rain! Kotmasu had come up to see us through it all. A queer figure in an out-of-date English mackintosh, the rubber as well as the style of which, he had admitted under pressure of my chaff, had perished, and a wonderful umbrella-like hat of huge diameter.

Down all the mountain-paths, and the steep roads leading into the town, the miniature torrents ran, as if they must sweep away the very foundations of the frail, queer-looking houses.

The harbour was blotted out, the town obscured by the vast grey masses of cloud, which, topping the hills they hid, seemed to fall down their sides into the hollow of the town.

Mousmé and I, till Kotmasu came, had watched the scene from the verandah, waiting for the rifts in the watery veil which, sure to come sooner or later, would give us exquisite peeps of indescribable loveliness.

Now all three of us are standing there in all the silver glory of Japanese moonlight.

Kotmasu even is silent, and makes no further attempt to explain English ways and customs to Mousmé.

The hillside, with its drenched foliage and grassy slopes, is like a sheet of frosted silver. In the foreground lies our garden set thick with Nature's flashing, gem-like rain-drops. The harbour can be seen again, as usual, an immense black pearl of irregular shape, with here and there a streak of moonlight pencilled on its tranquil surface. The cemeteries and tea-fields stretched below us to the right and left are but darker oxidised silver; the temples and tea-houses but embossed figures.

Down quite below us is the still darker patch of colouring, immense, far-spreading, which marks the town; the lights and the gleam of lanterns look in the damp air like angry eyes seen in tears.

Few sounds reach us, and even the cicala's chirp is far less noisy than usual. Mousmé still has hold of my hand, and I can see her face glancing upward now and then.

We might have remained there on the verandah with the light of the room behind us streaming out, a warm yellow patch, for another hour or two, so impressive was the view, and the silence which all three of us seemed so reluctant to break. But suddenly we are startled by the Boom! Boom—m—m! of the immense gong belonging to the Shinto monastery far below us down the mountain side. Such a noise!—awe-inspiring, terrific (if there be tone colours, then red, purple and orange), invading every hillside cranny, seeming positively to engulf us in its ever-widening air circles of sound.

"It has spoiled all," whispers Mousmé, heaving a sigh.

"Yes, little Mousmé. See, it has even frightened the moonbeams."

A dense cloud drags its edge across the face of the moon, and now all—except the lights of the town and the few twinkling, feeble lamps of the ships out in the harbour, which appear brighter suddenly for lack of their celestial rival—is dark.

Kotmasu knocks the ashes out of his tiny pipe bowl with a sharp, metallic tap upon the bamboo verandah rail, and says:

"There will be another storm soon. I must be going."

He says good-night somewhat reluctantly after all; and when we have watched him go away down the path, over the edges of which our poor rain-beaten tea-roses are straggling, with his big hat, paper umbrella on which a grinning and intelligent-looking red dragon is fearlessly daubed, and an orange paper lantern with bars and lozenges of vermilion, which the rising wind threatens every moment to overturn or extinguish, we go in.

Oka's wife is playing her samisen in the basement, its twanging strains ascending to us through the thin floor. She is singing now in a shrill, squeaky voice, perhaps to amuse Oka, or to lull one of the numerous little Okas to sleep. The song goes on to some accompaniment which is too irregular to be anything save an improvisation, all the time Mousmé is taking a few of the most valuable and elaborate pins out of her hair, preparatory to sleep. My toilet is a simple one compared to that of Mousmé, which indeed is so elaborate that I have frequently caught myself idly wondering why she ever gets up or goes to bed to go through such a process. There are her garments to be carefully stowed away in her little cupboards, curiously contrived behind the panelling. The proper folding of her obi is in itself a matter of some considerable importance, to judge from the serious, rapt expression of her face. Then there are the wonderful pins with which her pretty head, set so well on her sloping shoulders, is adorned.

There is no light to put out, because I always keep the lamp with its glowworm flame burning throughout the night. It permits, for one thing, Mousmé properly to arrange her head in the little hollow of her camphor-wood pillow; for another, it allows me to watch her fall asleep, and the antics of the moths outside our slate-blue gauze mosquito curtain when I cannot sleep myself.

To-night, however, I am lulled to rest by the sheer monotony of Oka's wife's song; and the last thing I remember is the twang, twing, twang of her samisen, which is quite loud now, I have my ear so close to the floor.

Chapter X

This morning we have had a visit from mother-in-law and the little monkey of an Aki. It appears that Kotmasu has told her—and what is more, has made her at last believe—that we are really going away to England.

Mother-in-law is unlearned except in the housekeeper's art, and this conveys nothing very definite as regards locality to her mind. England, Europe even, is as indefinite a place as the Shinto heaven. Somewhere out beyond the harbour, which she can see from our verandah, even beyond green-wooded Hoyaki and Cape Nomo, but that is all she knows or can imagine. We are going away, therefore she will not be the further recipient of the "handsome presents" in which her soul delights. I quite comprehend that this is the direction her thoughts will take, and it is really to assure herself that Kotmasu's statement is absolutely true that she has toiled up the hillside in the hot sun so early in the day.

Why she has brought Aki to the family council I cannot conceive; but Aki has brought a tortoise about the size of a silver dollar, with which he contentedly plays in the sun on the verandah, where I can see his funny little shaven head, with its tufts of black hair, bobbing about, above the edge of the lower half of our sliding-panel window as we talk. No doubt he has brought some fantastically shaped and gorgeously coloured doughtoy out from the folds of his outer garment to keep the tortoise company.

"So you are going away?" says mother-in-law in Japanese, Mousmé's efforts to teach her even a few words of English having proved quite unavailing.

"Yes," I reply; "we are going to England soon."

I somehow feel as though I were committing a robbery; and her next remark serves rather to deepen my disquietude.

"You are going to take my daughter with you, honourable sir?"

"Yes."

"I thought you would only require her whilst you remained in Nagasaki."

I have never yet succeeded in making my mother-in-law understand the permanency of my attachment, and I do not hope to accomplish the feat now; but I explain, hinting that there will be "handsome presents" to all the members of her (for me inconveniently large) household when we take our departure.

This, if nothing else, she comprehends; and she offers no further objection to Mousmé's accompanying me.

In many respects I like this queer little painted doll of a mother-in-law, who has really wonderfully beautiful brown hair, and a childish way and smile, notwithstanding her seven children, and underlying native rapacity on a small and engagingly frank scale. So I suggest that Mousmé and I shall give a farewell entertainment to my Japanese relations, and this idea meets with her most cordial approval.

I smile to myself at having mollified her so easily, and reflect that, as Kotmasu once philosophically remarked, marriage was cheaper after all, and I should have no cash payment to make for permission to take Mousmé with me.

Mother-in-law is quite content now, and as firmly convinced as ever that I am a "velly much rich honourable English sir," for thus Oka always describes me. She insists upon prostrating herself most outrageously, to the disarrangement of her obi, on the end of which she unfortunately steps when she takes her leave, which she does as soon as she is satisfied that it is really my intention to ask all my relations to a farewell fête.

Mousmé is, I fancy, a little alarmed at the prospect; for as soon as her mother has gone with Aki weeping at her side, and apparently refusing to be comforted by his mother's more or less specious promises, because of the disappearance of his tortoise, which has doubtless fallen down amongst Oka's progeny through a crack in the verandah floor, she exclaims in an awe-struck voice:

"Cy-reel, do you know how many there are?"

"No," I am forced to admit.

"They are as numerous as the bees in the garden."

"Very well," I answer resignedly; "we must do our best."

"They are very strange, some of them, very strange persons indeed," she continues, with a look of surprise that I am not frightened.

"The more bees, the greater the honey," I reply, quoting a maxim that may be hers, or her mother's, or one of national adoption.

Her little face—perhaps she is dreading all the fuss and bother and pain of taking leave of people she may care for—becomes more sober than ever.

"But there is a barber!"

I exhibit no surprise.

She takes my hand to prepare me for the last and greatest shock of all.

"Cy-reel, I am afraid that there may be a sampan boy."

This is coming down in the world with a vengeance. But what are the odds? So I reassure her.

"Mother is sure to let it be known. Perhaps, even, people who are not relations may come, people I should not care to know," resumed Mousmé, drawing herself up, and looking ridiculously funny in her sudden affectation of pride—and after the sampan man, too!

I shall have a queer party, it is certain. Never mind. Only, I must caution Mousmé not to mention her uncle the barber to Lou when we get to England, nor refer even casually to the brother-in-law who earns a living as a sampan rower.

During the next few days Mousmé is very busy. She knows, if I do not, what a superior and lavish entertainment will be expected of the "very much rich English sir;" men and women from the town seem to be clicking our wicket gate after them all day long, and walking up the path to the house interminably.

Mousmé has ordered everything which can in any way assist in confirming their belief in my importance and wealth. The piéces de résistance of the feast are different sorts of Huntley and Palmer's biscuits. I know well how little Aki's eyes will gleam at the mere sight of the sugared ones.

These biscuits, strange to say, will stamp the entertainment as one of superior character. They are, of course, very dear, and Mousmé knows they will be duly appreciated.

She tells me in an awed voice that her numerous relatives will come early and depart late.

"Will, perhaps, not go until all these wonderful biscuits have disappeared."

I smilingly pretend to be very terrified.

We have entertained our vast collection of relatives; and possibly more than one stranger unawares.

What a quaint conglomeration they proved! How they all could be related still puzzles me; but related undoubtedly most of them were, from "gilded youths" (some of Mousmé's numerous cousins-in-law) in their bowler hats and other pseudo-European garments, with the silly faces of idlers, to the much-feared sampan rower, who proved quite a gentleman in manners.

Mousmé and I received them, and listened to their profuse compliments, whilst I, at least, was inwardly amused at their salutations and kow-towing, performed even by the ladies on all-fours.

Oka and his wife hand round tiny cups of tea, equally minute plates of candied beans, plums in sugar, and cherries in vinegar; and as our guests' tastes are satisfied, they pass out into the garden, gay with lanterns, and full of music performed by some strolling samisen players whose services I secured.

These really play well. If only they would not sing!

My numerous relatives are in no hurry to go. But at length, quite late, the last family has left us, with their lanterns in their hands and reiterated good wishes and compliments on their lips; and the garden is again silent save for the chirruping cicalas, who, like the poor, are indeed always with us, the splash of the fountains, and the hoarse, sepulchral croak, croak of awakened frogs.

We linger, Mousmé and I, a little while in the garden, which at the end of the month we shall give over into other hands, and then we go in, and Mousmé smokes a little pipe ere retiring to rest. It took me some time to get accustomed to the habit, which seems to afford her such unqualified delight, but now I am resigned. The tobacco is so mild, and the little silver pipe with its thimble-sized bowl looks so toy-like and innocent; and now I find, from the papers and magazines Lou sends me, that it is becoming quite the fashion for women and girls in England to smoke mild and scented cigarettes sub rosa.

Mousmé knocks out the ashes from her pipe on the edge of her little ember bowl, with a metallic pin, pin, pan, and then, taking off her day garment of plum-coloured brocade, slips into a dressing-gown robe of blue linen, with wide sleeves and an obi of powder-blue muslin, which she knots in the inevitable exaggerated butterfly bow round her supple waist.

I shall, after all, be sorry to leave this strange Eastern home of mine, with its queer noises at the dead of night, and its fragrant garden, the sweet perfume from which drifts in and even penetrates through our blue mosquito-curtain of stout gauze, when we leave, as we frequently do, the panels of our outer wall pushed back for air.

Then there is the trouble of packing; the bother of going through all the letters and papers which I at first, when home-sick, commenced to keep because they came from home, and afterwards because I was too indolent to destroy them. All this must be done now, however; must indeed be begun to-morrow. There are Mousmé's belongings, too, which she is already packing in her mind's eye in ridiculous little lacquer boxes, which would be battered into matchwood ere they were stowed in the hold.

I lie awake for some time thinking over all this, and watching the big night-moths come in through the open panel of the window, and then flutter round the idol's head for a moment ere singeing their poor soft wings at the flame of the lamp burning before its placid features. Some of them are so big that they make quite an appreciable noise on the white matting floor when they fall headlong on to it. I fall asleep watching—

"the deadly gyrations of the poor fascinated things, on suicide intent,"

and dream that I am pursued by huge monsters of moths with heads like the awful masks I see every day in the curio shops. And I frighten little Mousmé nearly out of her wits, just as it is getting light, by my frantic attempts to escape from my dream-bred horrors, and the environment of the mosquito-curtain.

When I am fully awake we sit bolt upright on our mattress bed, and laugh just like children; I because Mousmé, with face screwed up in half-laughter, half-tears, looks so comical with her eyes blinking at the light; and she because it is such a relief for her to find that "Cy-reel is not gone mad after all."

Mousmé and I spent the first part of the day shopping, buying Japanese curios and native silks and embroideries for those at home, a very expensive cabinet with whole nests of tiny drawers for Lou—frankly, to propitiate her—and European articles when and where we could get them for the "handsome presents" of which my mother-in-law and Mousmé's numerous brothers and sisters are so fond.

Mousmé's dress is an ideal one for such an amusement as shopping. It is simply astounding how much she can stow away mysteriously in the many pockets of her wide sleeves alone.

Down at Ako San's, the jeweller, near the quay, whose shop is a general dépôt for things European, she packs away, I can scarce conceive where, half the numerous little purchases we make. I take the rest; and then loaded, both of us, arms, pockets and all, we slowly climb the hill to our home, which is already partially dismantled in view of our departure.

It has that terrible, painful vacancy of a house half-deserted. It seems no longer to belong to us, as though the ghosts of possible future tenants already possessed it. Poor tiny house, which will probably know Mousmé's laugh no more!

Whilst Mousmé is wrapping up our presents in soft, silky textured rice-paper ready for their recipients, I get together some of my things.

Alas! when I come to sort my clothing, I am made painfully aware that when I land in England I shall be shabby and out-of-date.

There is a whole pile of European clothing on the floor near my writing-table, the sunlight cruelly exposing all its shabbiness; but little of it will be of use. I shall give some of the best of the garments remaining when I have selected mine, to Mousmé's two elder brothers. They will be delighted even if the things don't fit. They possess minds happily unvexed by such momentous questions as "bagging at the knees" and "a bad fit about the back and shoulders." Happy Japanese mashers!

At last I have persuaded Mousmé that her toy trunks and lacquer boxes are no use for travelling to England. She has never had anything else, and can scarcely understand why they will not do.

I have bought her, through the kind agency of Kotmasu (who is up with us nearly all day long, now that we are going to leave so soon), a big trunk—a veritable Saratoga, I fondly believe—which had belonged to a deceased lady missionary. Into this trunk, with infinite care, Mousmé is placing all her little belongings, packed for double security in the lacquer boxes, with storks, frogs and fishes decorating them, which I had condemned.

Really, Mousmé has quite a respectable amount of luggage.

This will be something in her favour at any rate in sister Lou's eyes. What a gorgeous little fairy she will look in all her fantastic finery!

A possible new owner of the house has been here this morning; and although he was terribly polite and ridiculous in his lengthy-phrased humility and repeated prostrations, he did not succeed in dispelling the impression all possible new owners seem to create, namely, that the old owner is an intruder whose presence is only by sufferance, though his lease may not have actually expired. This attitude of this one—the man about to take possession—is a bit of human nature; the same, I found, in Japan as elsewhere.

We finish our packing at sunset.

Nothing now remains visible in our bare-stripped home except the things we retain for our use, which will be packed in confusion at the moment of departure.

We fully intended to go down to the great tea-house to-night for the last time; but although we both say we are too tired, we are in truth both aware that we have no heart for mixing with the merry throng, or for watching the geishas dancing. So we go to rest.

"Our last night here," as Mousmé says, with a little choked sob. Everything is now described as "last."

It is terribly melancholy.

In the morning we go round the garden, and Mousmé gathers a posy of the choicest flowers, pink-cupped lotus, gardenias and roses; she buries her face in it to hide the tears I know are falling in salt dew upon the fragrant blossoms. Then we feed the gold-fish, and watch them poke their red-gold heads just above the surface, making rippling circles which widen and rock the lily-leaves and lotus blossoms. And whilst we are doing all this in the sunlit garden of our late home, we can hear Oka's deep, gruff voice giving directions to the men who, with dilapidated rikishas now turned into hand-trucks, are loading up our luggage to take it down to the quay and on board the steamer.

"That is the last," we hear Oka say in gruff tones; "mind that the honourable English sir's effects are not damaged."

"Yes, that is the last," says one of the porters.

"This is the last," says Mousmé, opening her hand over the gold-fish pond.

We go up the path to the house in silence; look sorrowfully into each of the bare, empty rooms; take leave of Oka, and Oka's wife, who is in tears; press a shining new yen into each of the innumerable children's hands, even into that of the brown baby in Oka's wife's arms, whose tiny fist is not large enough to hold the shining silver, in which it sees only a new plaything; and then walk away out of the garden of sweet flowers to follow our porters with the luggage.

Next morning we are to sail soon after sunrise, and we get up to see the last of Nagasaki and our home, now a mere matchbox-looking villa (when seen from the deck of our steamer down here in the harbour) perched high up on the hillside, in company with scores of other similar abodes.

As we drift out from our moorings in mid-harbour, we catch sight of it for the last time, and Mousmé through her tears kisses her fingers to it.

We wave our hands and handkerchiefs to those on shore, to Kotmasu, a tiny figure on the quay, and to the men who have congregated in their sampans, like a flock of water-fowl, to see the great jokisen off.

Then we pass through the narrow neck of the harbour, with the towering green slopes of the hills seeming almost about to fall on top of us, past Hoyaki, out into the ocean beyond.

Mousmé, who stands by my side all the time, her hand clutching my arm, gives a shuddering little sob.

Who can blame her?

With every throb of the engines, every heave of the huge vessel to the ocean swell, we are carried farther and farther into the—for her—unknown.

And it is only the unknown which is terrible.